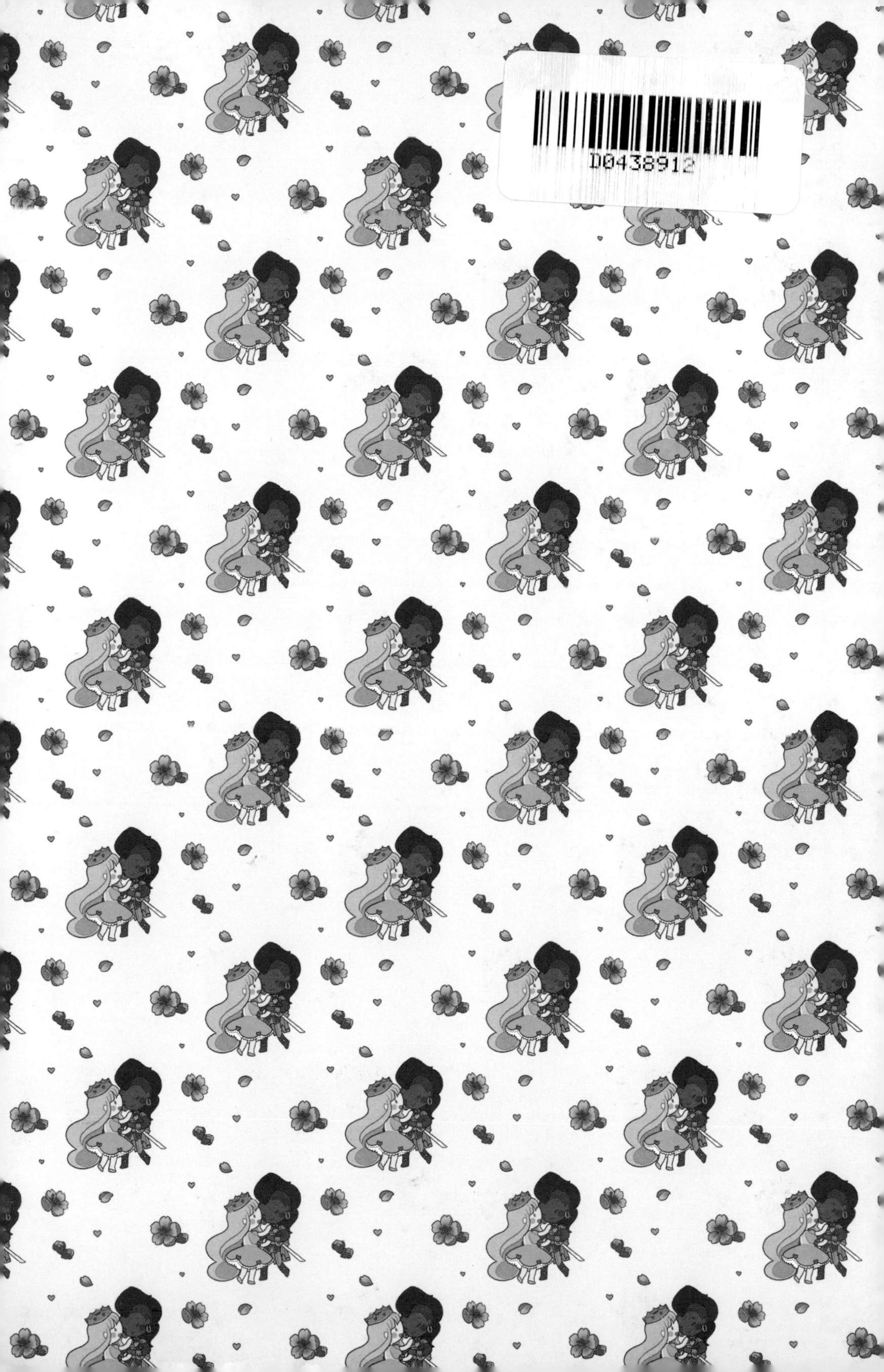

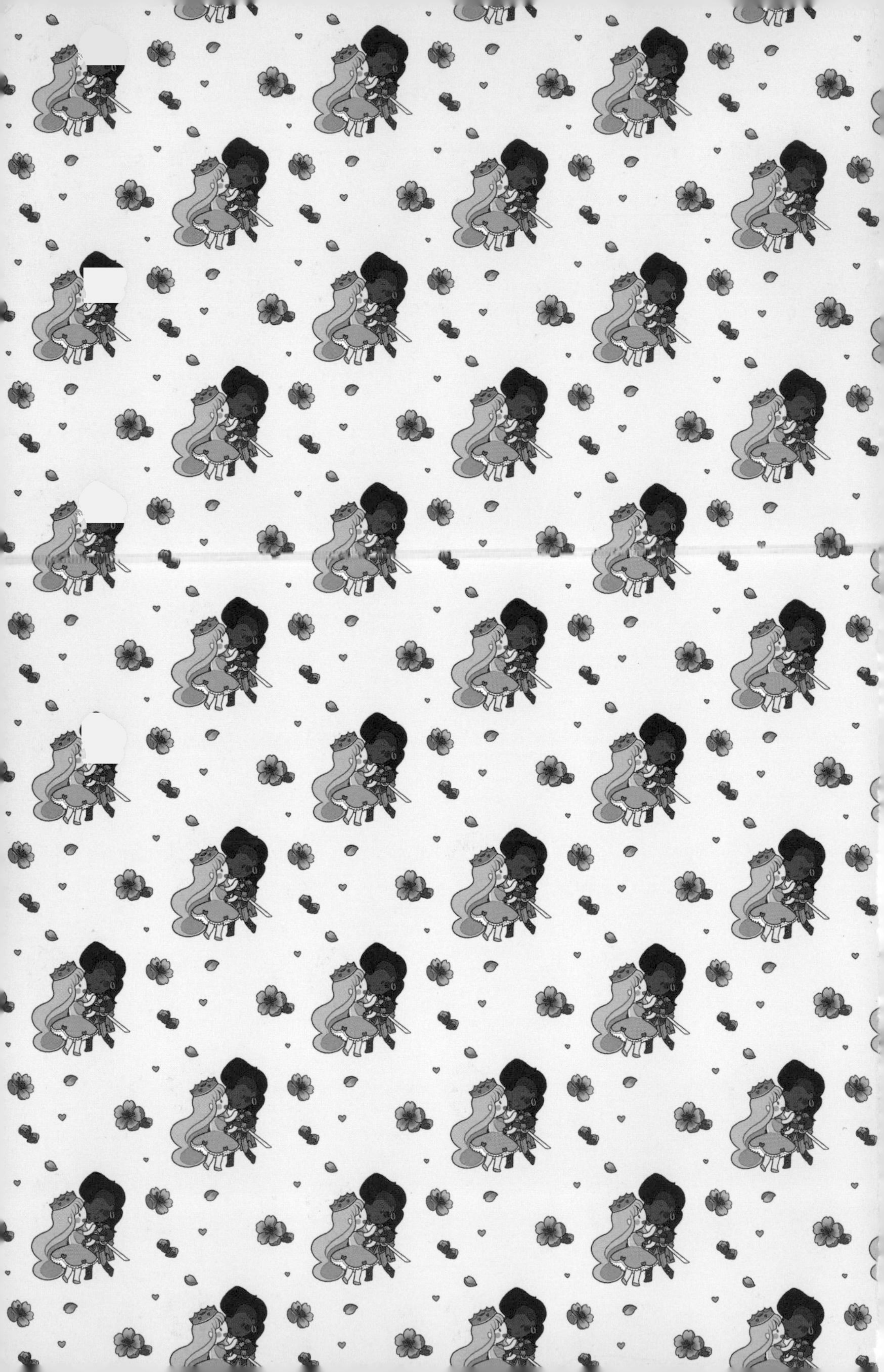

PRINCESS PRINCESS
Ever After

PRINCESS PRINCESS
Ever After

By KATIE O'NEILL

Edited by Ari Yarwood
Designed by Fred Chao

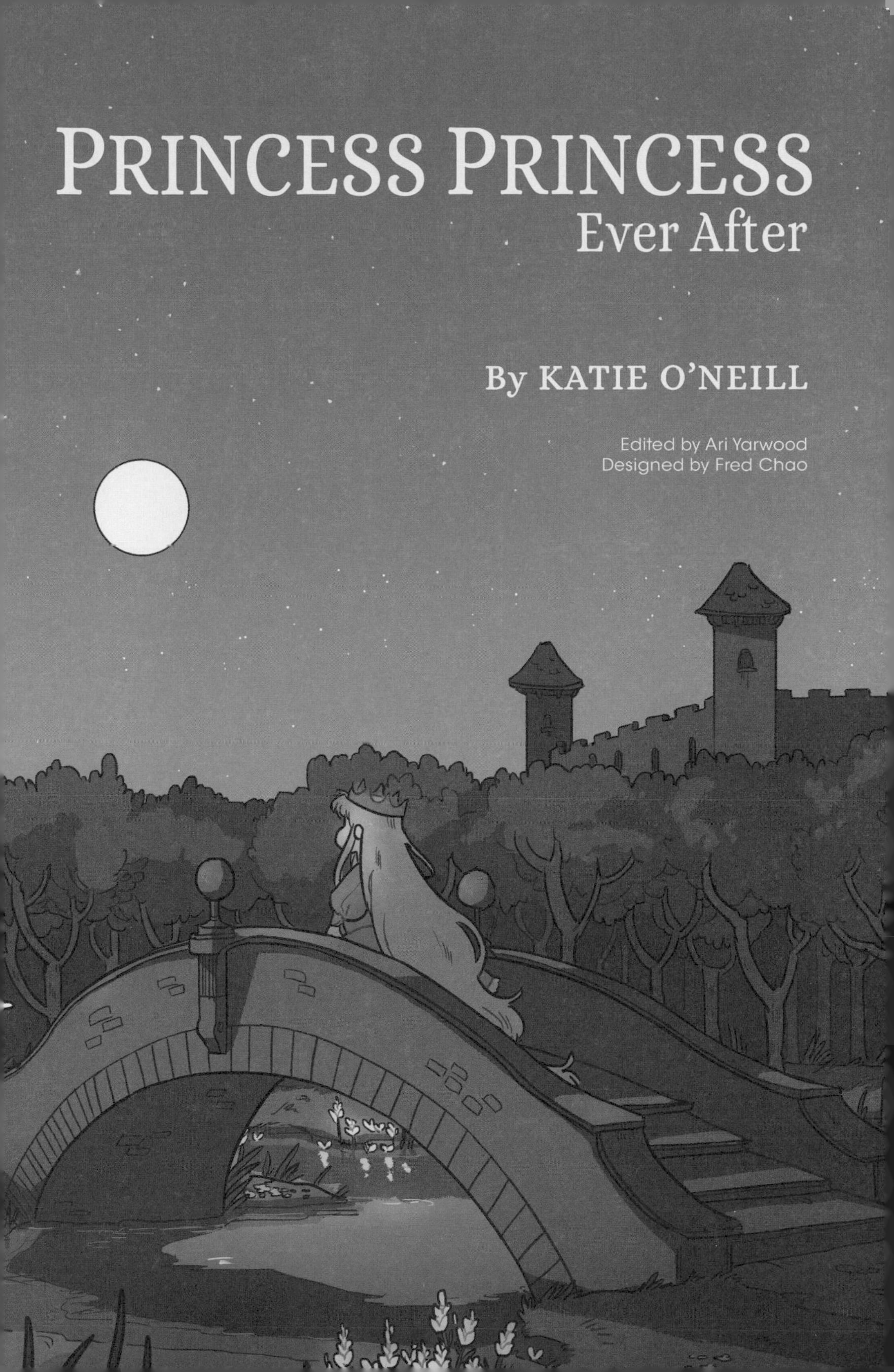

Published by Oni Press, Inc.
Joe Nozemack, publisher
James Lucas Jones, editor in chief
Andrew McIntire, v.p. of marketing & sales
Cheyenne Allott, director of sales
Rachel Reed, publicity coordinator
Troy Look, director of design & production
Hilary Thompson, graphic designer
Jared Jones, digital art technician
Ari Yarwood, managing editor
Charlie Chu, senior editor
Robin Herrera, editor
Bess Pallares, editorial assistant
Brad Rooks, director of logistics
Jung Lee, logistics associate

onipress.com
facebook.com/onipress
twitter.com/onipress
onipress.tumblr.com

strangelykatie.com
twitter.com/strangelykatie
strangelykatie.tumblr.com

Endpaper design by Sarah Ahn

First Edition: September 2016

ISBN 978-1-62010-340-1
eISBN 978-1-62010-341-8

Printed in Singapore

Library of Congress Control Number: 2016931407

3 4 5 6 7 8 9 10

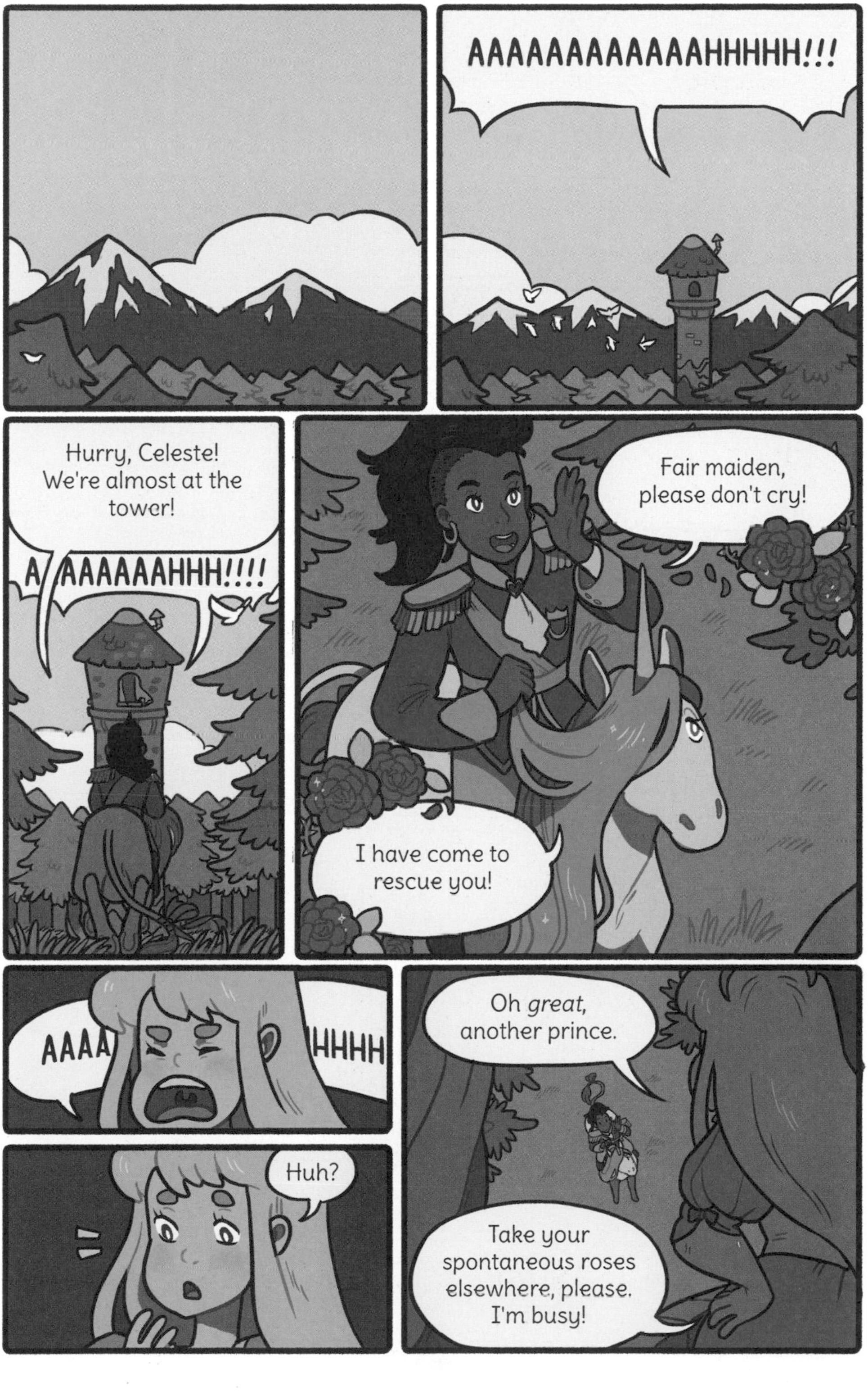
AAAAAAAAAAAAHHHHH!!!
Hurry, Celeste! We're almost at the tower!
AAAAAAAHHH!!!!
Fair maiden, please don't cry!
I have come to rescue you!
AAAA HHHH
Huh?
Oh *great*, another prince.
Take your spontaneous roses elsewhere, please. I'm busy!

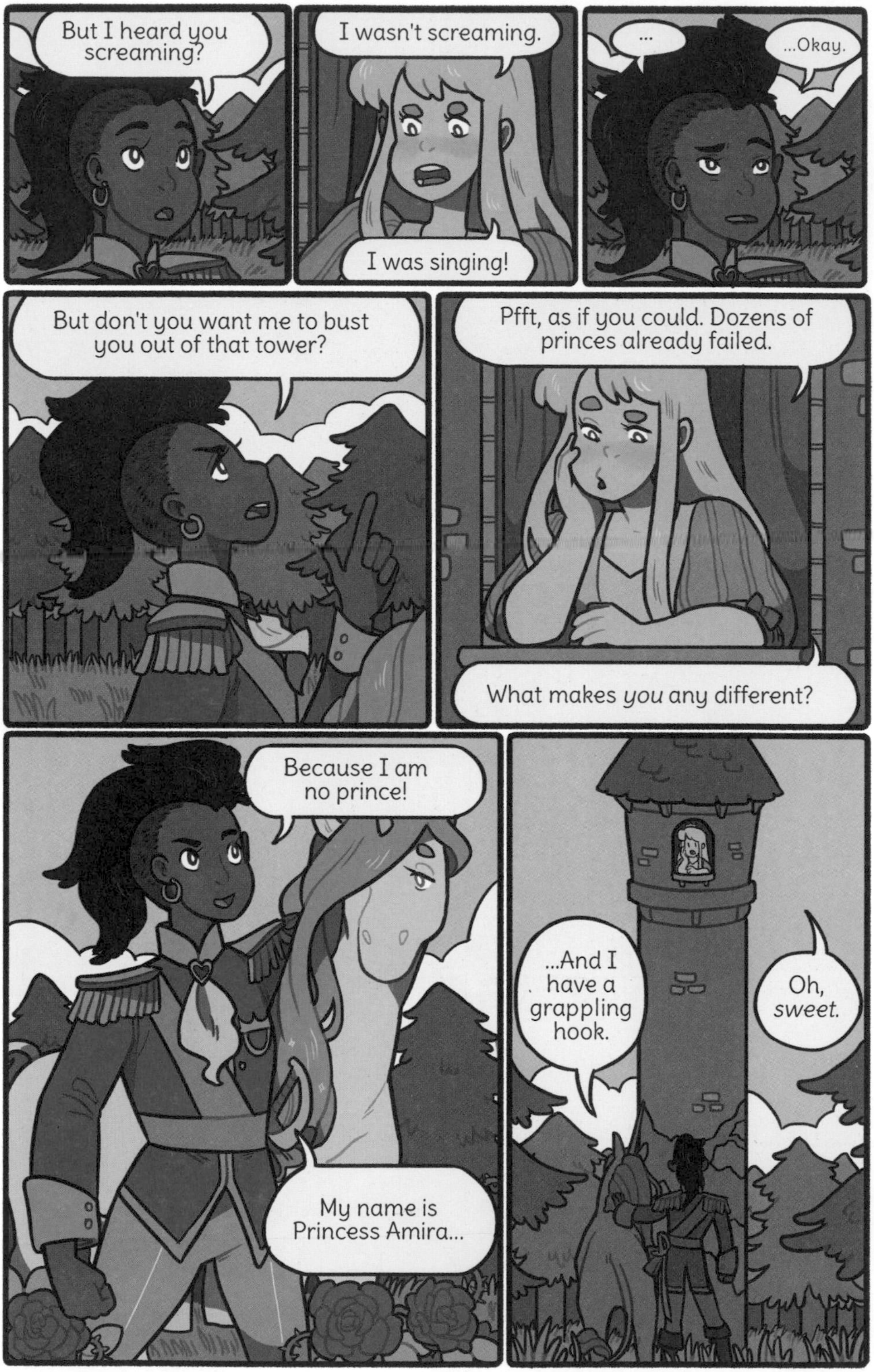

But I heard you screaming?
I wasn't screaming.
I was singing!
...
...Okay.
But don't you want me to bust you out of that tower?
Pfft, as if you could. Dozens of princes already failed.
What makes *you* any different?
Because I am no prince!
My name is Princess Amira...
...And I have a grappling hook.
Oh, *sweet.*

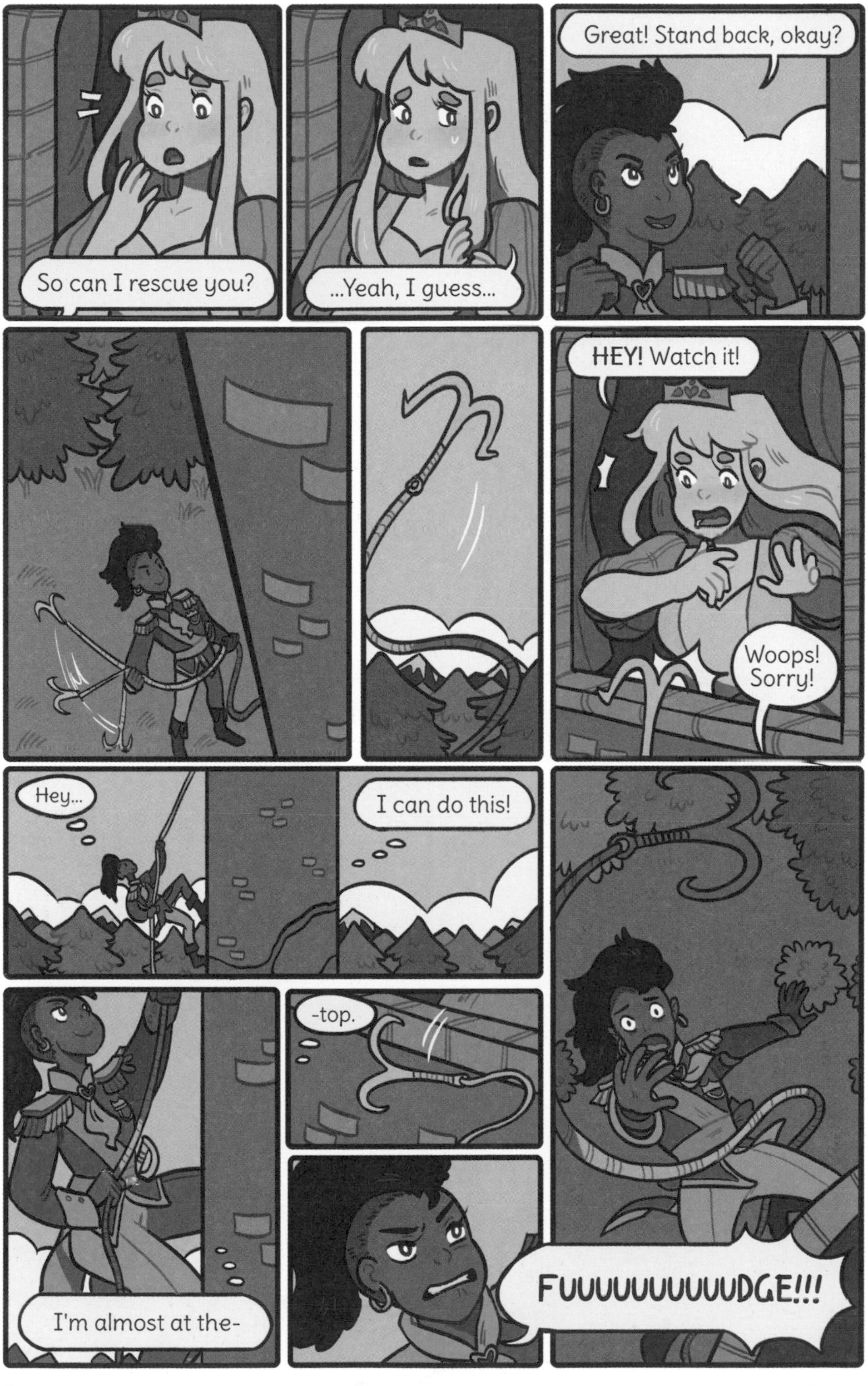
So can I rescue you?
...Yeah, I guess...
Great! Stand back, okay?
HEY! Watch it!
Woops! Sorry!
Hey...
I can do this!
I'm almost at the-
-top.
FUUUUUUUUUUDGE!!!

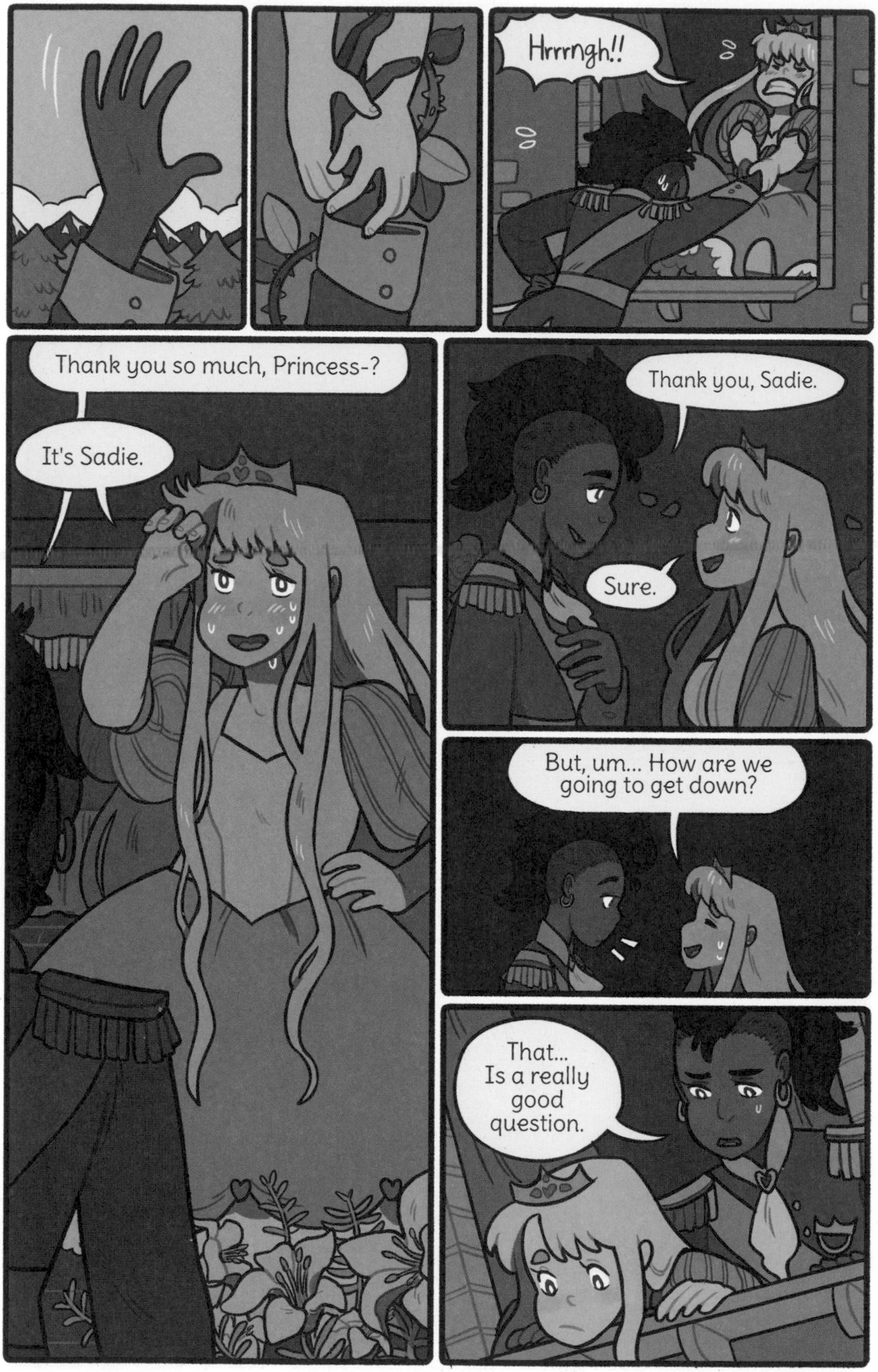

Hrrrngh!!
Thank you so much, Princess-?
It's Sadie.
Thank you, Sadie.
Sure.
But, um... How are we going to get down?
That... Is a really good question.

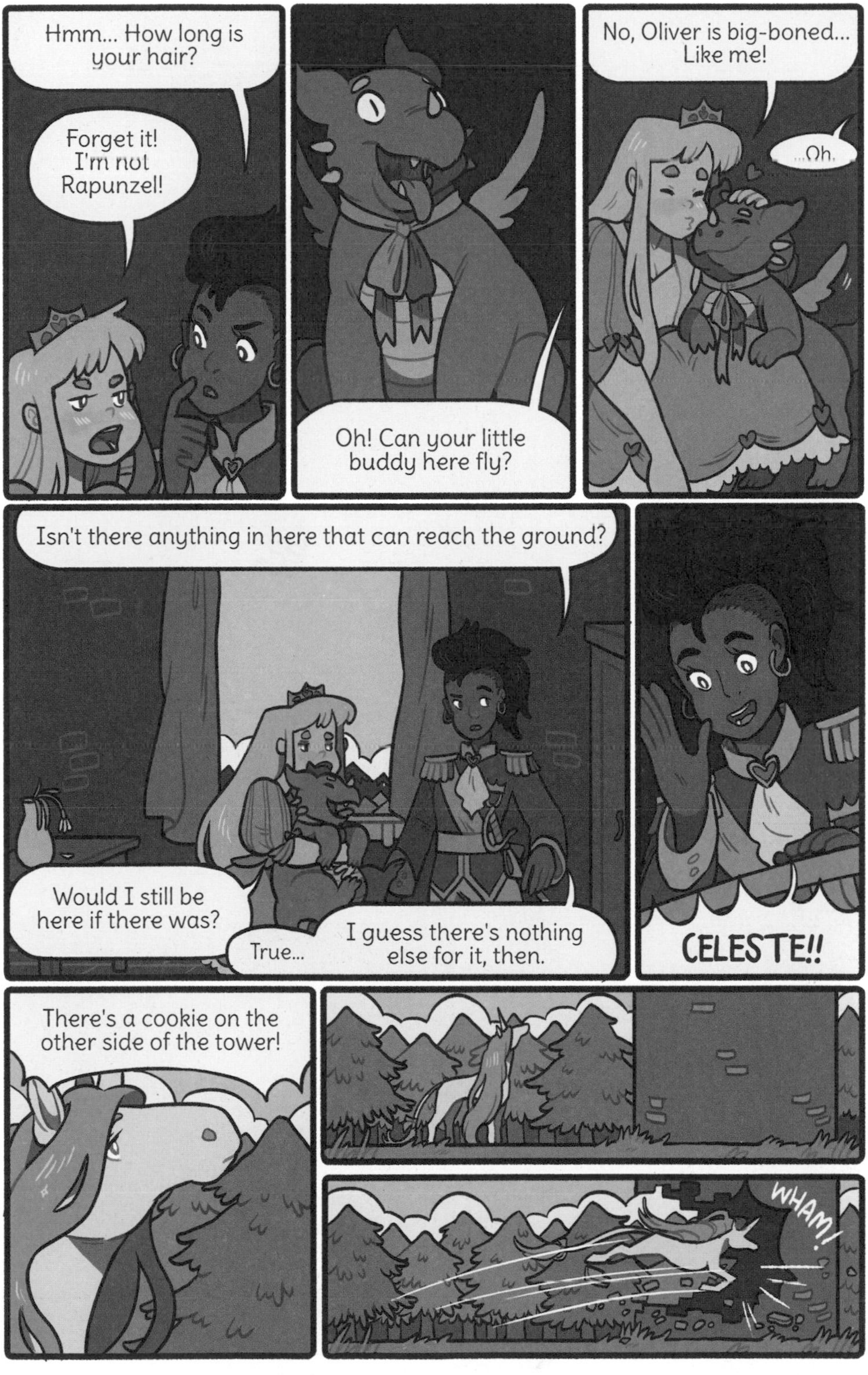
Hmm... How long is your hair?
Forget it! I'm not Rapunzel!
Oh! Can your little buddy here fly?
No, Oliver is big-boned... Like me!
...Oh.
Isn't there anything in here that can reach the ground?
Would I still be here if there was?
True...
I guess there's nothing else for it, then.
CELESTE!!
There's a cookie on the other side of the tower!
WHAM!

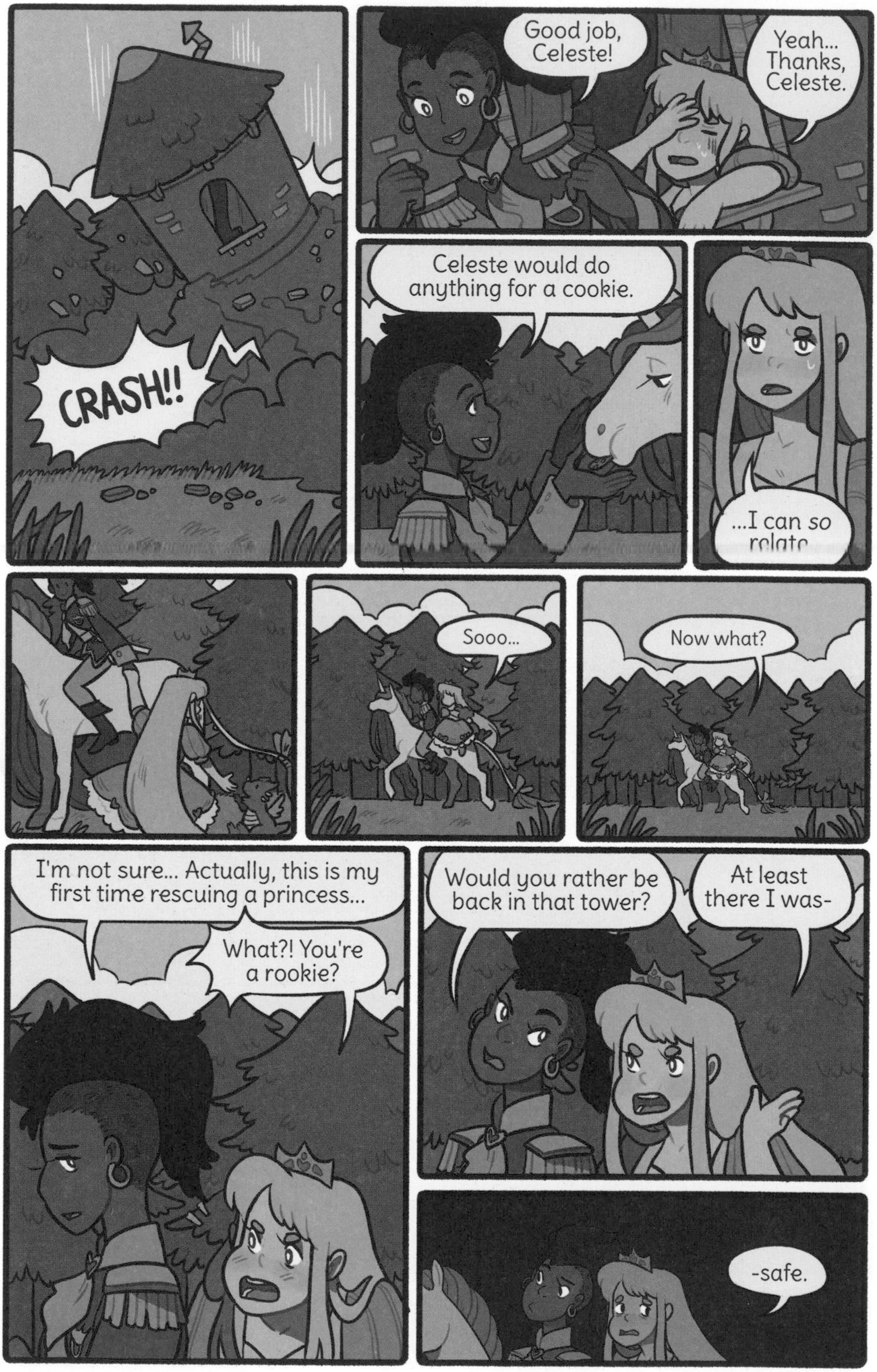
CRASH!!
Good job, Celeste!
Yeah... Thanks, Celeste.
Celeste would do anything for a cookie.
...I can so relate.
Sooo...
Now what?
I'm not sure... Actually, this is my first time rescuing a princess...
What?! You're a rookie?
Would you rather be back in that tower?
At least there I was-
-safe.

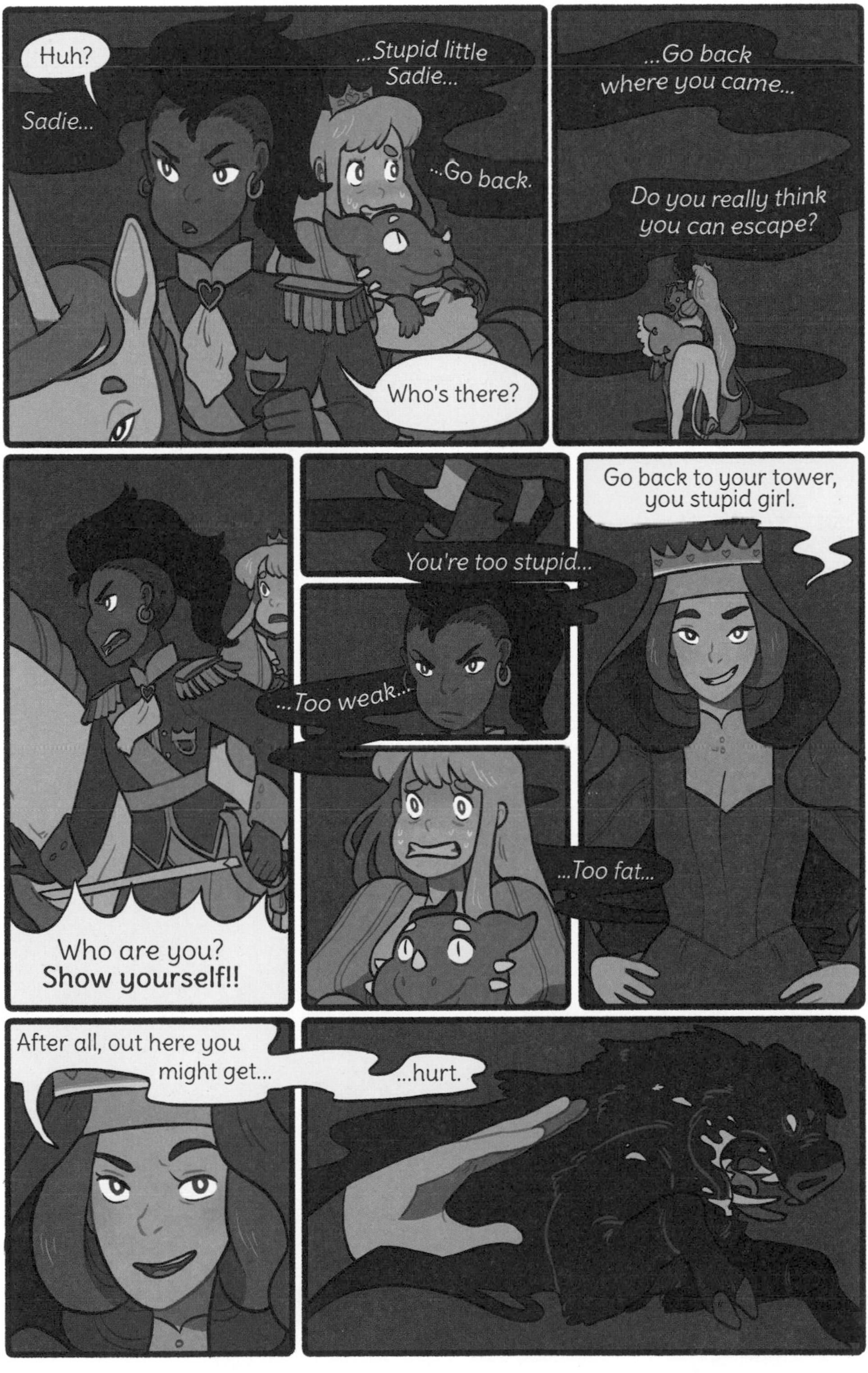
Huh?
Sadie...
...Stupid little Sadie...
...Go back.
Who's there?
...Go back where you came...
Do you really think you can escape?
Who are you? **Show yourself!!**
You're too stupid...
...Too weak...
...Too fat...
Go back to your tower, you stupid girl.
After all, out here you might get...
...hurt.

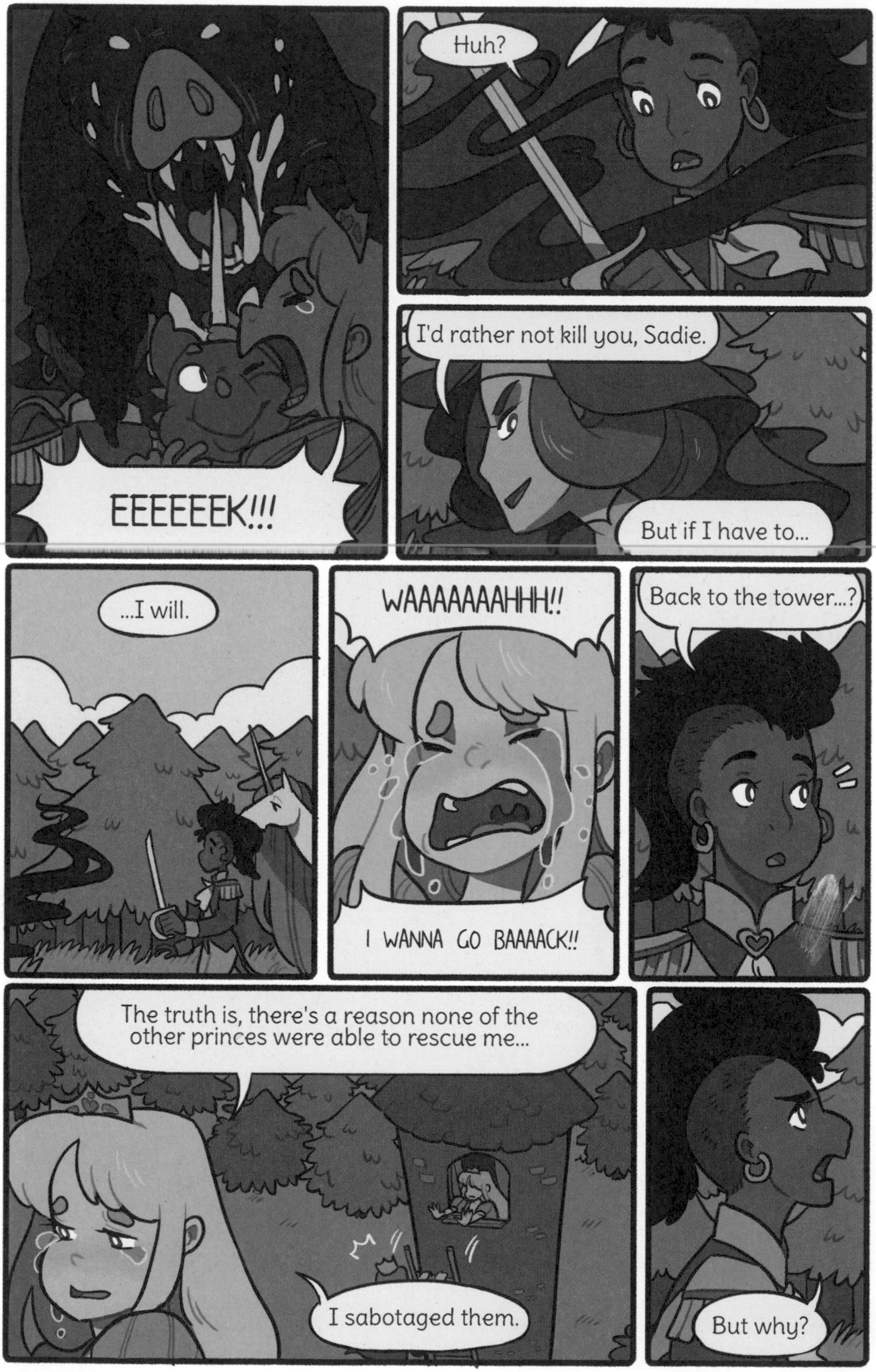
EEEEEEK!!!
Huh?
I'd rather not kill you, Sadie.
But if I have to...
...I will.
WAAAAAAAHHH!!
I WANNA GO BAAAACK!!
Back to the tower...?
The truth is, there's a reason none of the other princes were able to rescue me...
I sabotaged them.
But why?

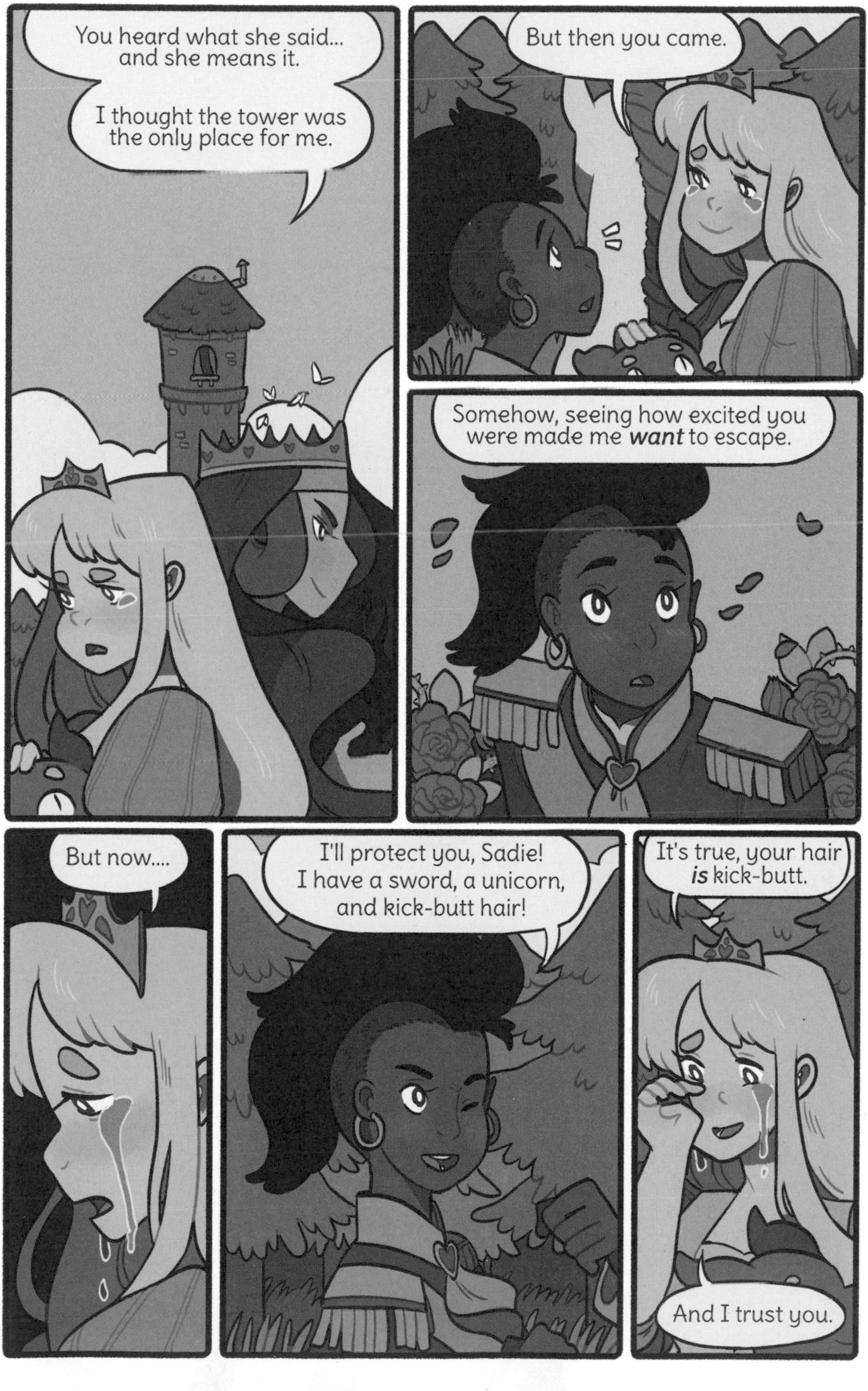
You heard what she said... and she means it.
I thought the tower was the only place for me.
But then you came.
Somehow, seeing how excited you were made me *want* to escape.
But now....
I'll protect you, Sadie! I have a sword, a unicorn, and kick-butt hair!
It's true, your hair *is* kick-butt.
And I trust you.

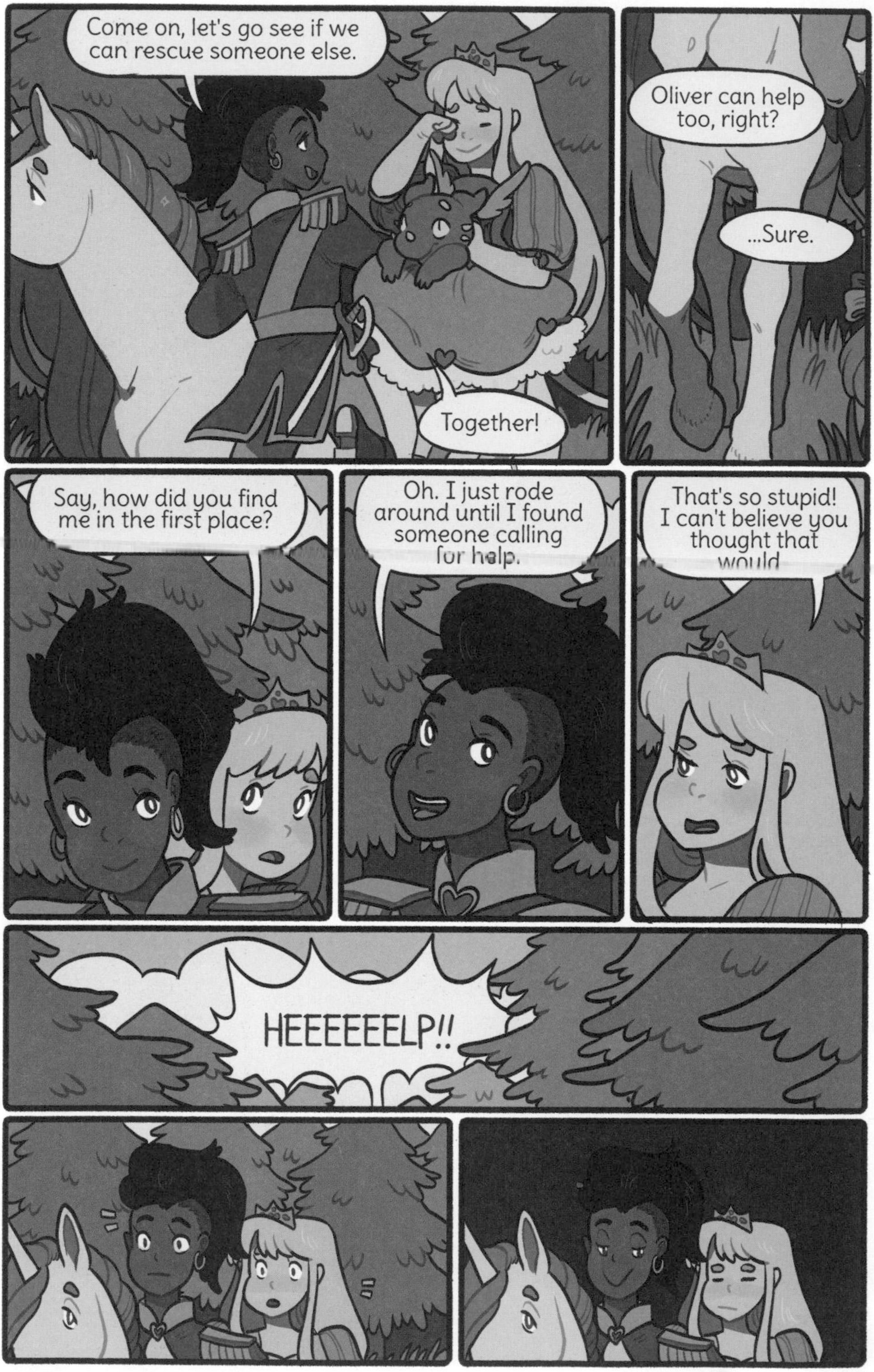
Come on, let's go see if we can rescue someone else.
Together!
Oliver can help too, right?
...Sure.
Say, how did you find me in the first place?
Oh. I just rode around until I found someone calling for help.
That's so stupid! I can't believe you thought that would
HEEEEEELP!!

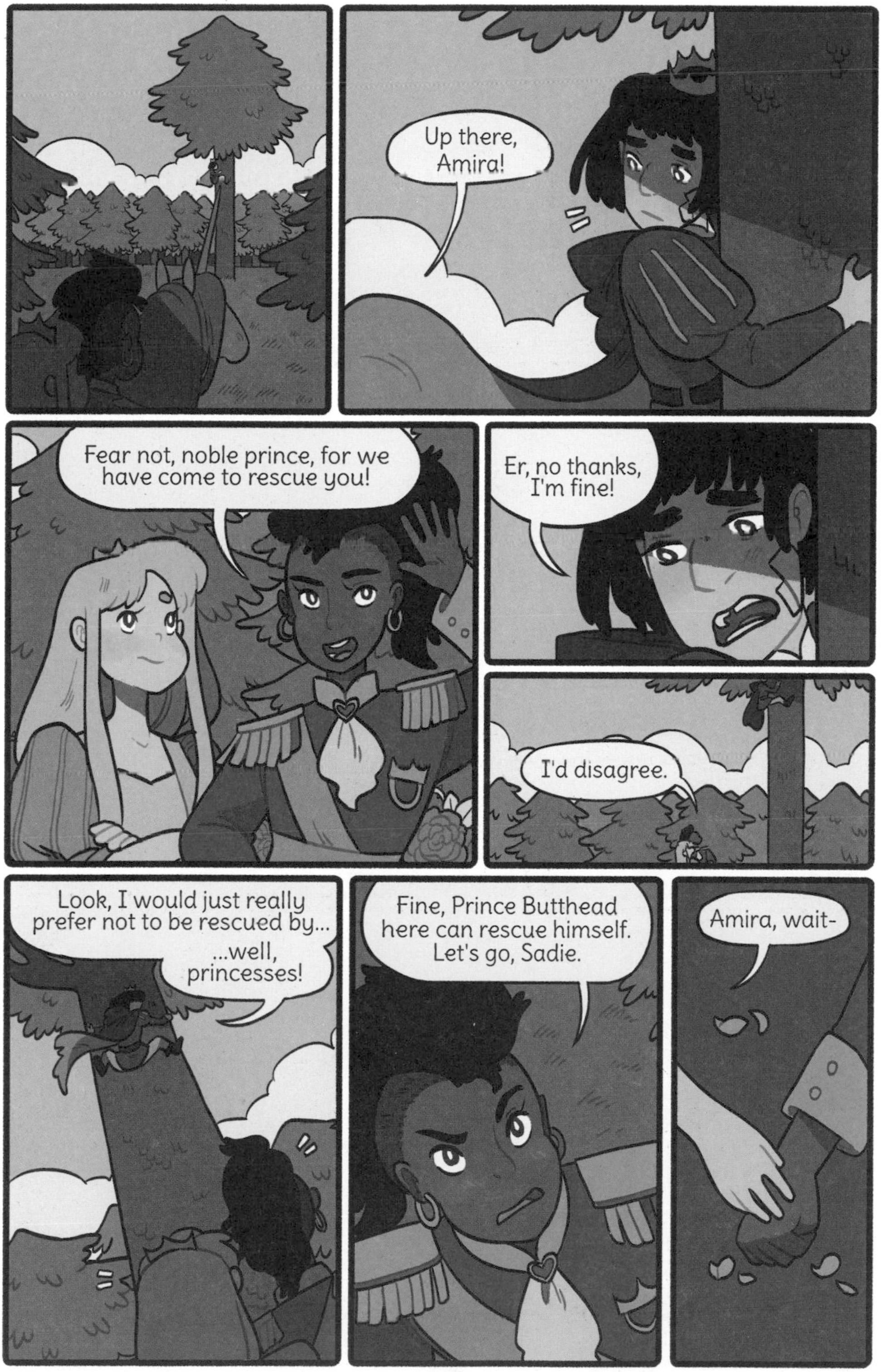
Up there, Amira!
Fear not, noble prince, for we have come to rescue you!
Er, no thanks, I'm fine!
I'd disagree.
Look, I would just really prefer not to be rescued by...
...well, princesses!
Fine, Prince Butthead here can rescue himself. Let's go, Sadie.
Amira, wait-

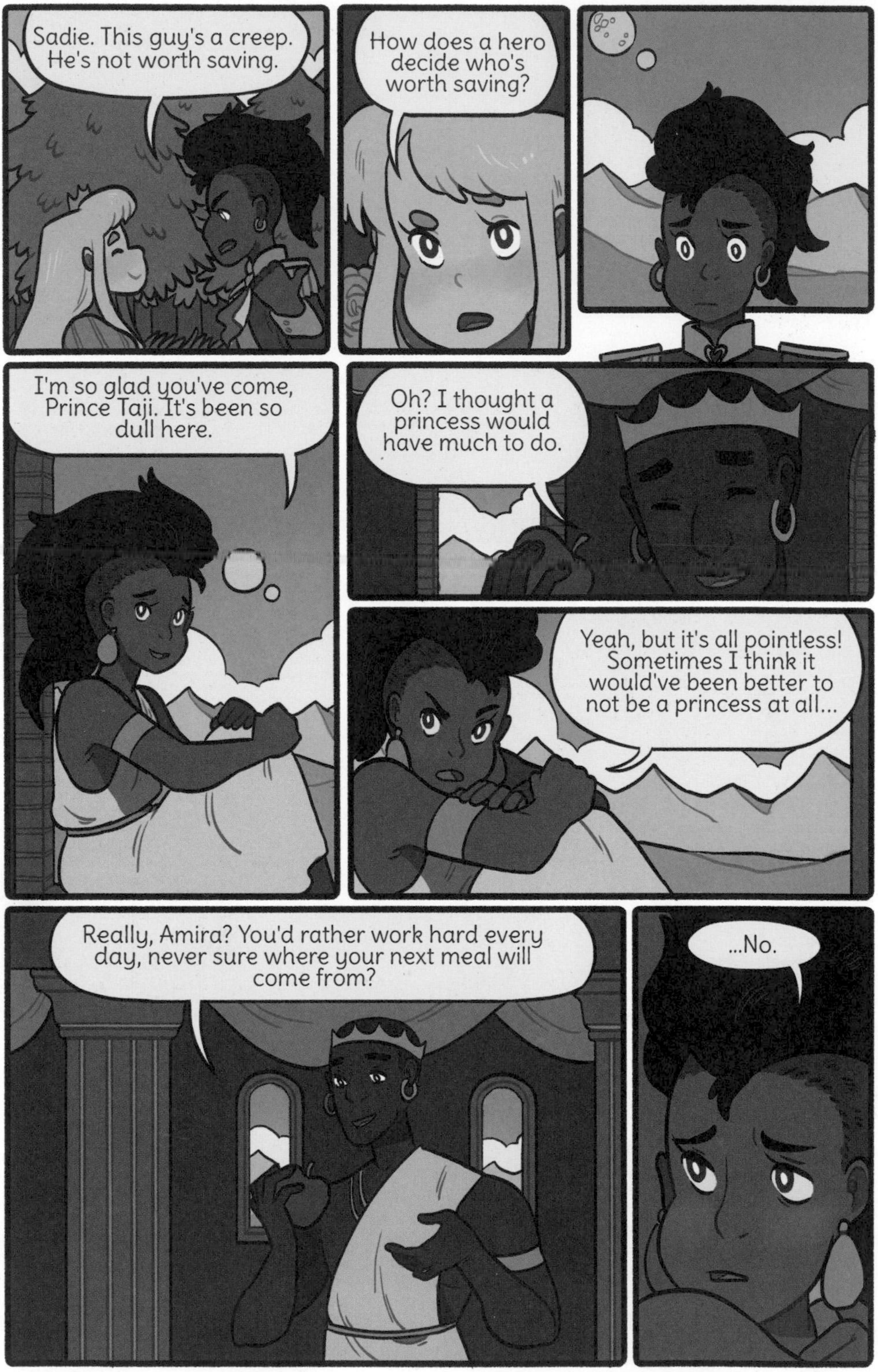
Sadie. This guy's a creep. He's not worth saving.
How does a hero decide who's worth saving?
I'm so glad you've come, Prince Taji. It's been so dull here.
Oh? I thought a princess would have much to do.
Yeah, but it's all pointless! Sometimes I think it would've been better to not be a princess at all...
Really, Amira? You'd rather work hard every day, never sure where your next meal will come from?
...No.

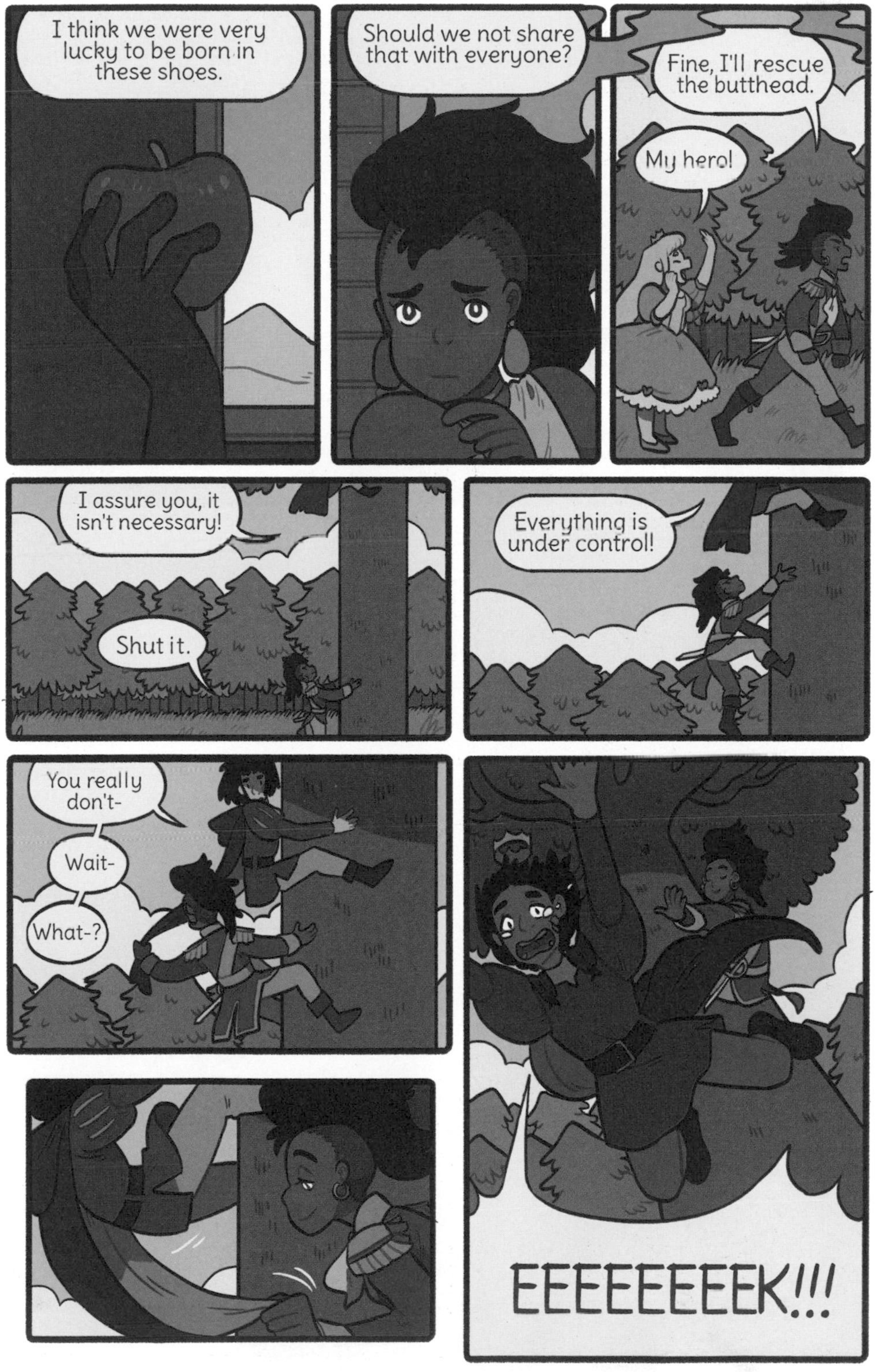
I think we were very lucky to be born in these shoes.
Should we not share that with everyone?
Fine, I'll rescue the butthead.
My hero!
I assure you, it isn't necessary!
Shut it.
Everything is under control!
You really don't-
Wait-
What-?
EEEEEEEEK!!!

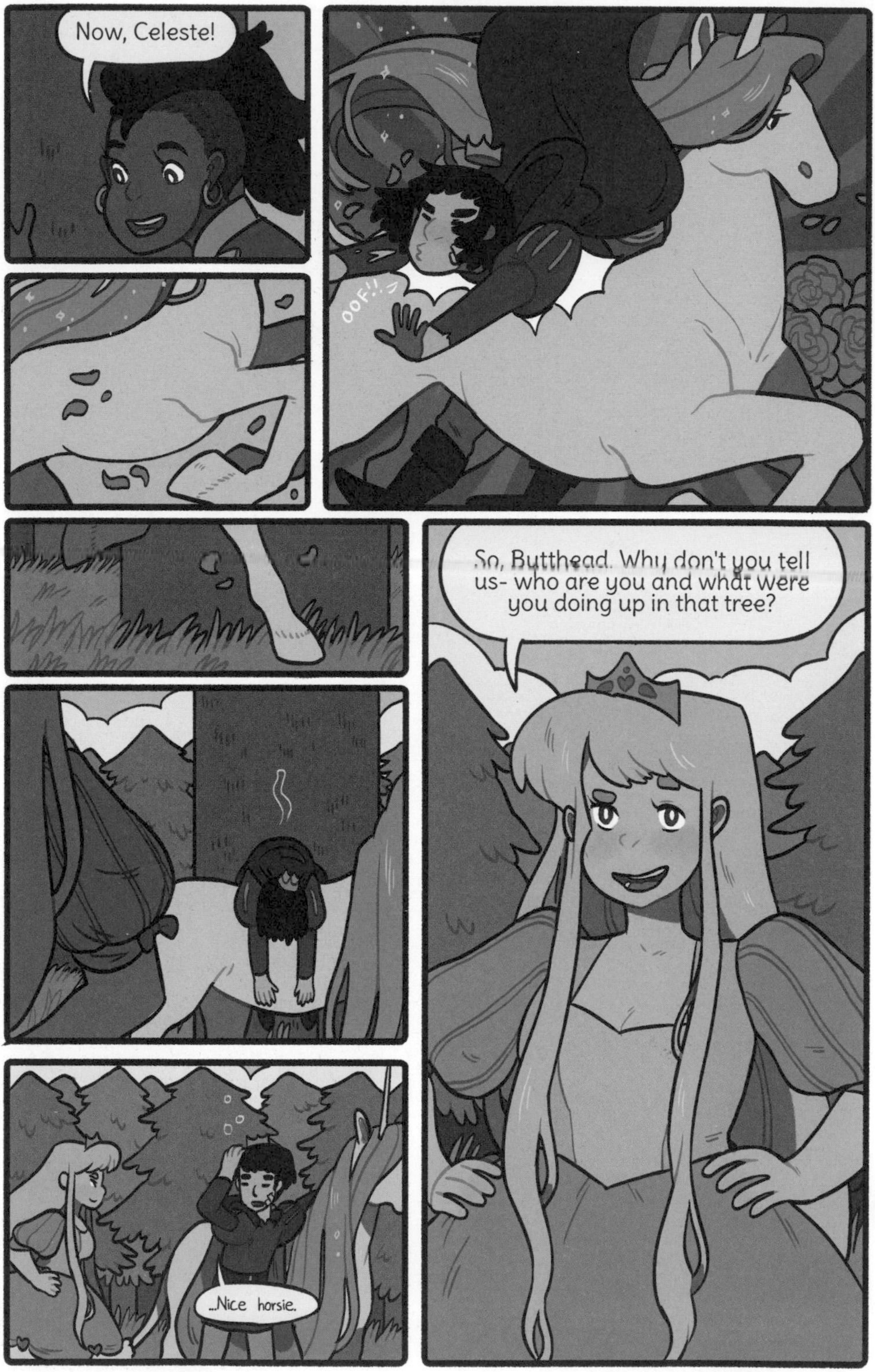
Now, Celeste!
OOF!!
So, Butthead. Why don't you tell us- who are you and what were you doing up in that tree?
...Nice horsie.

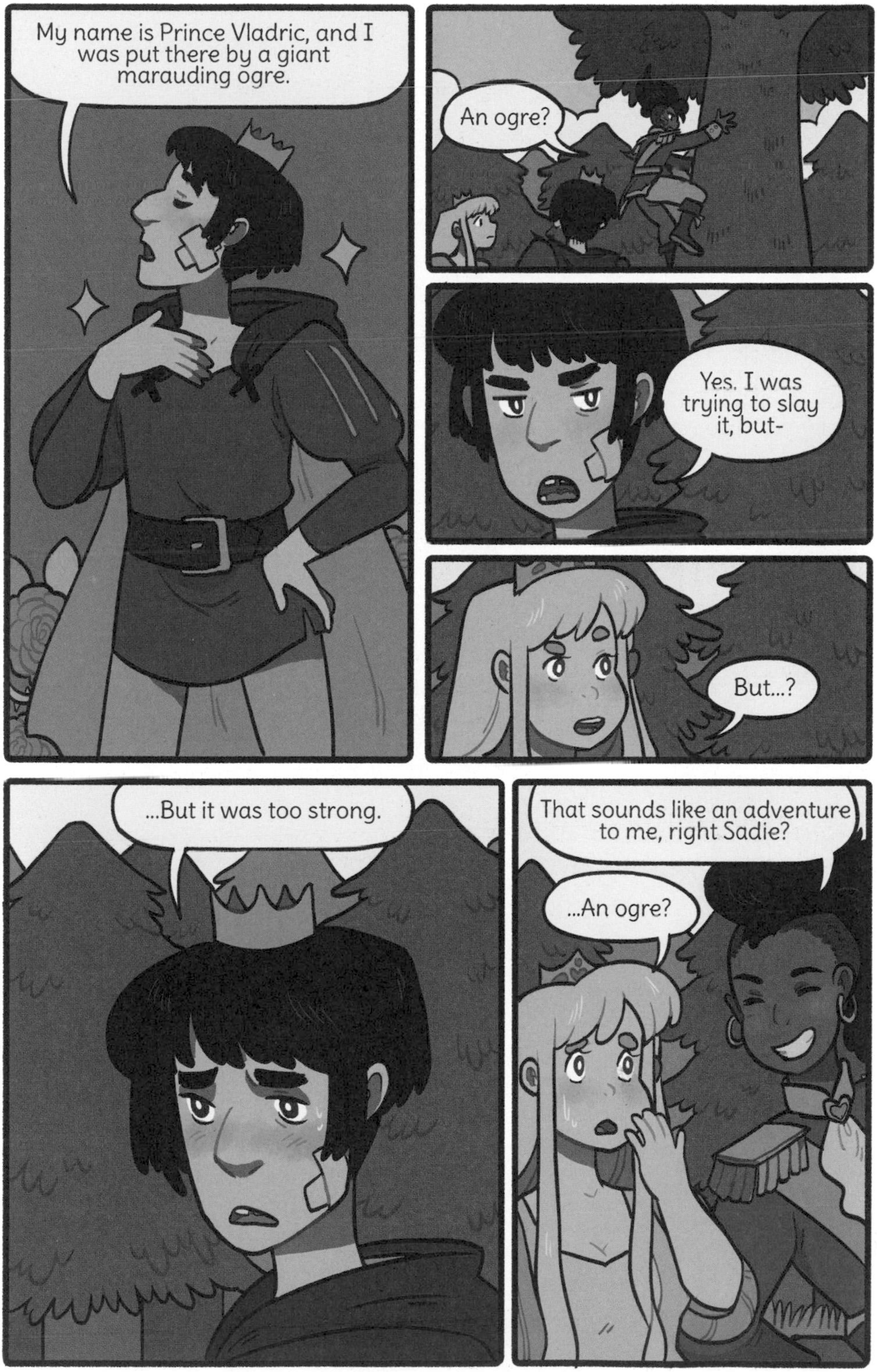
My name is Prince Vladric, and I was put there by a giant marauding ogre.
An ogre?
Yes. I was trying to slay it, but-
But...?
...But it was too strong.
That sounds like an adventure to me, right Sadie?
...An ogre?

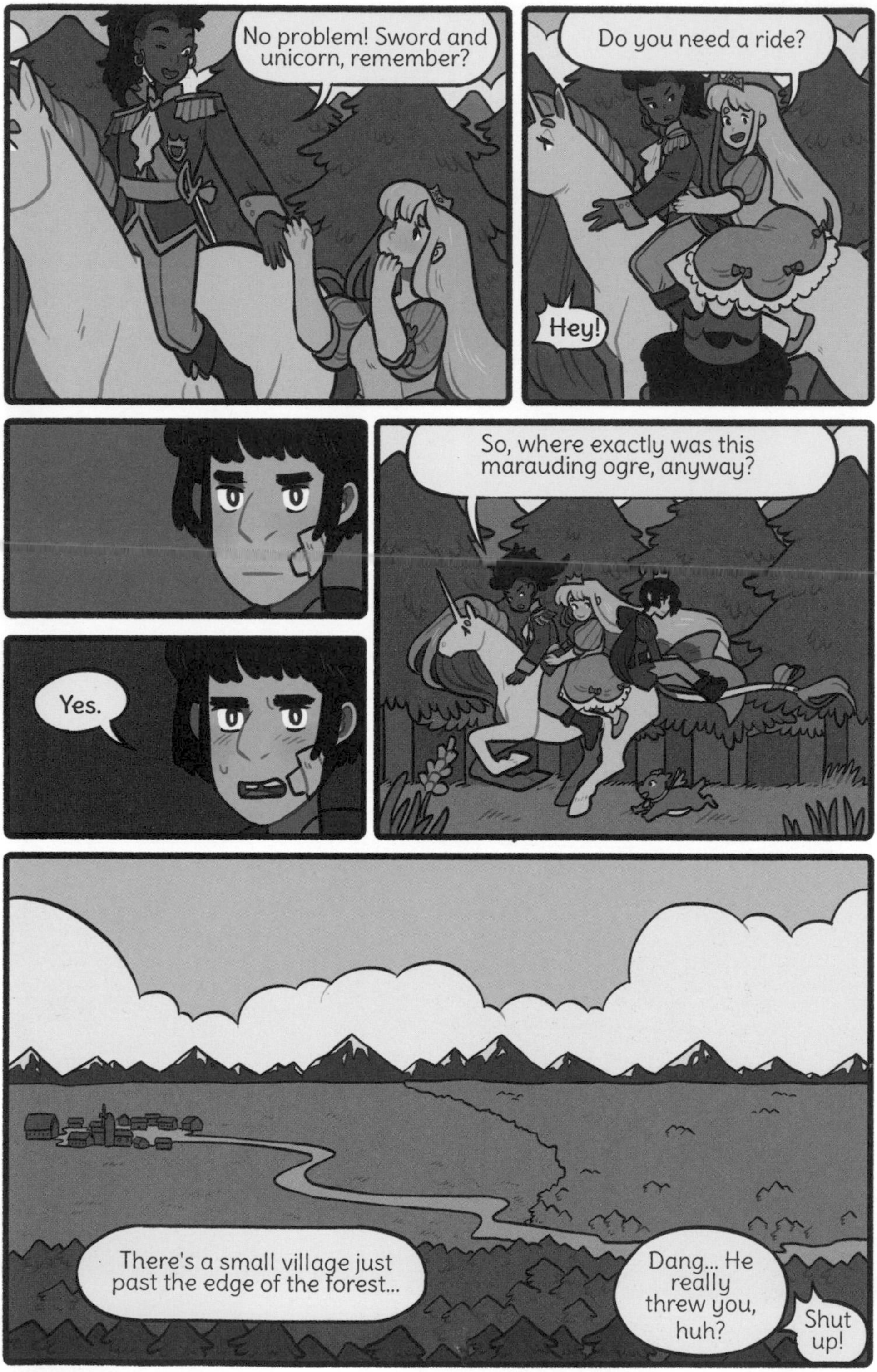
No problem! Sword and unicorn, remember?
Do you need a ride?
Hey!
Yes.
So, where exactly was this marauding ogre, anyway?
There's a small village just past the edge of the forest...
Dang... He really threw you, huh?
Shut up!

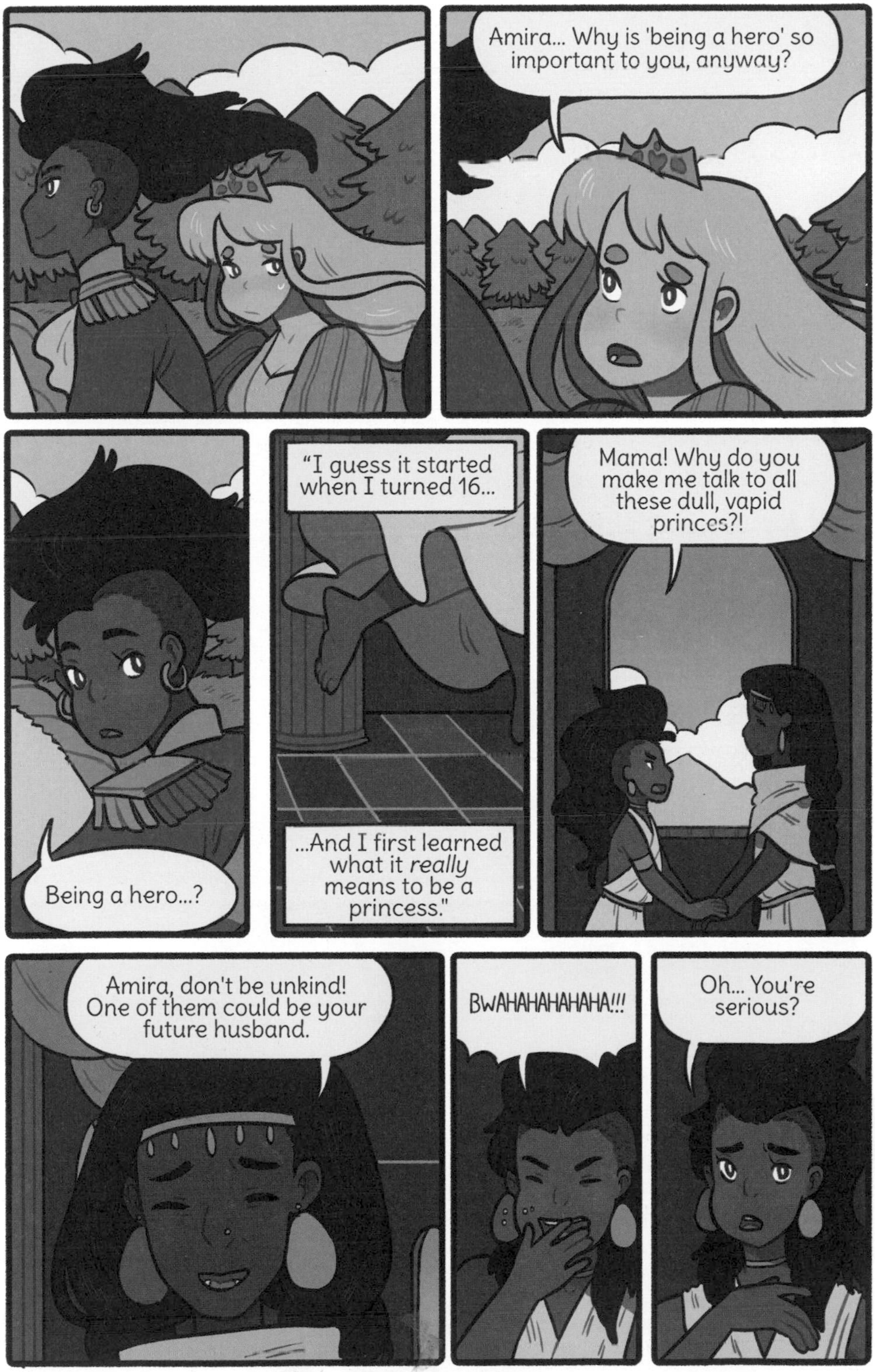
Amira... Why is 'being a hero' so important to you, anyway?
Being a hero...?
"I guess it started when I turned 16...
...And I first learned what it *really* means to be a princess."
Mama! Why do you make me talk to all these dull, vapid princes?!
Amira, don't be unkind! One of them could be your future husband.
BWAHAHAHAHAHA!!!
Oh... You're serious?

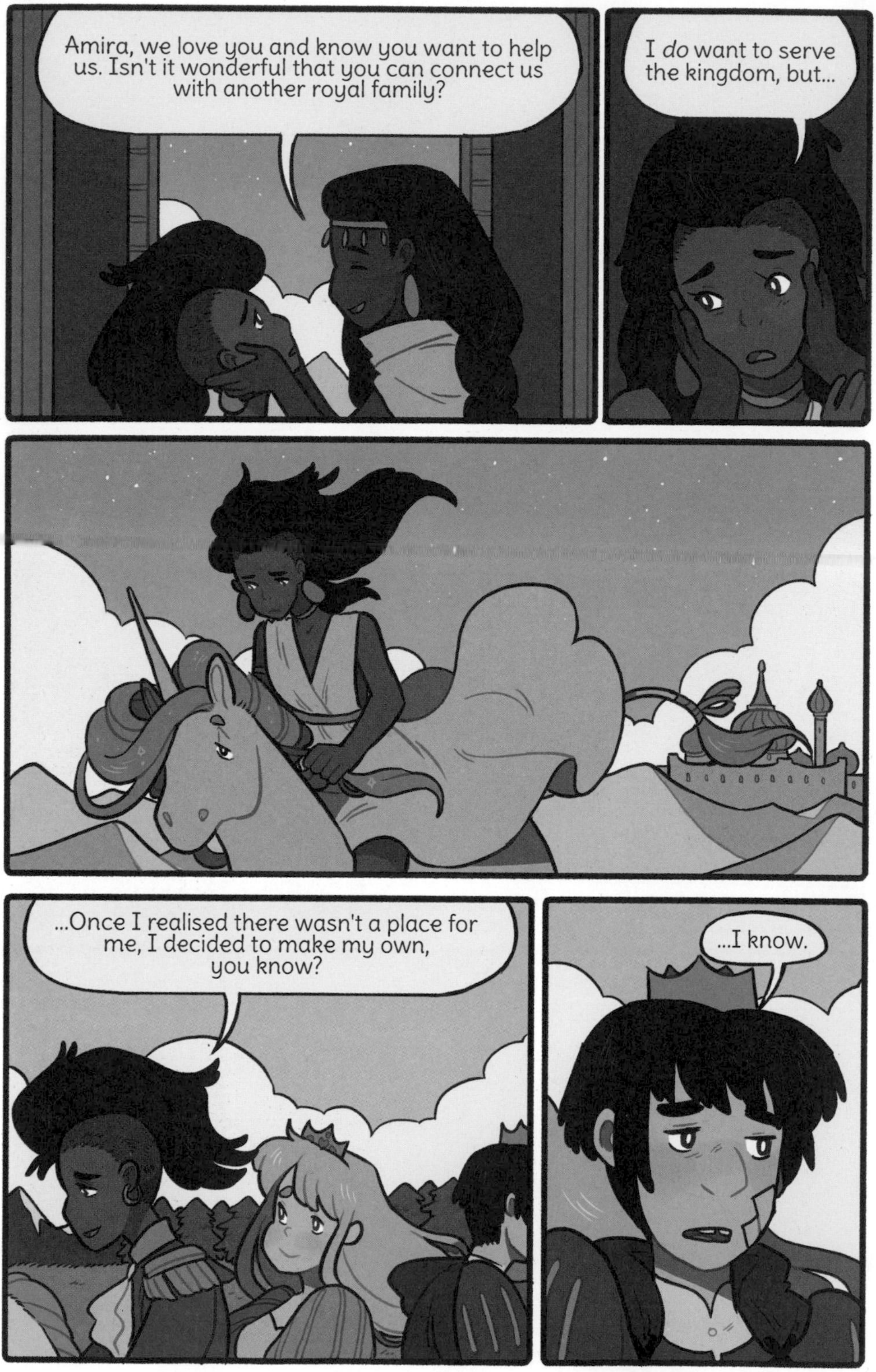
Amira, we love you and know you want to help us. Isn't it wonderful that you can connect us with another royal family?
I *do* want to serve the kingdom, but...
...Once I realised there wasn't a place for me, I decided to make my own, you know?
...I know.

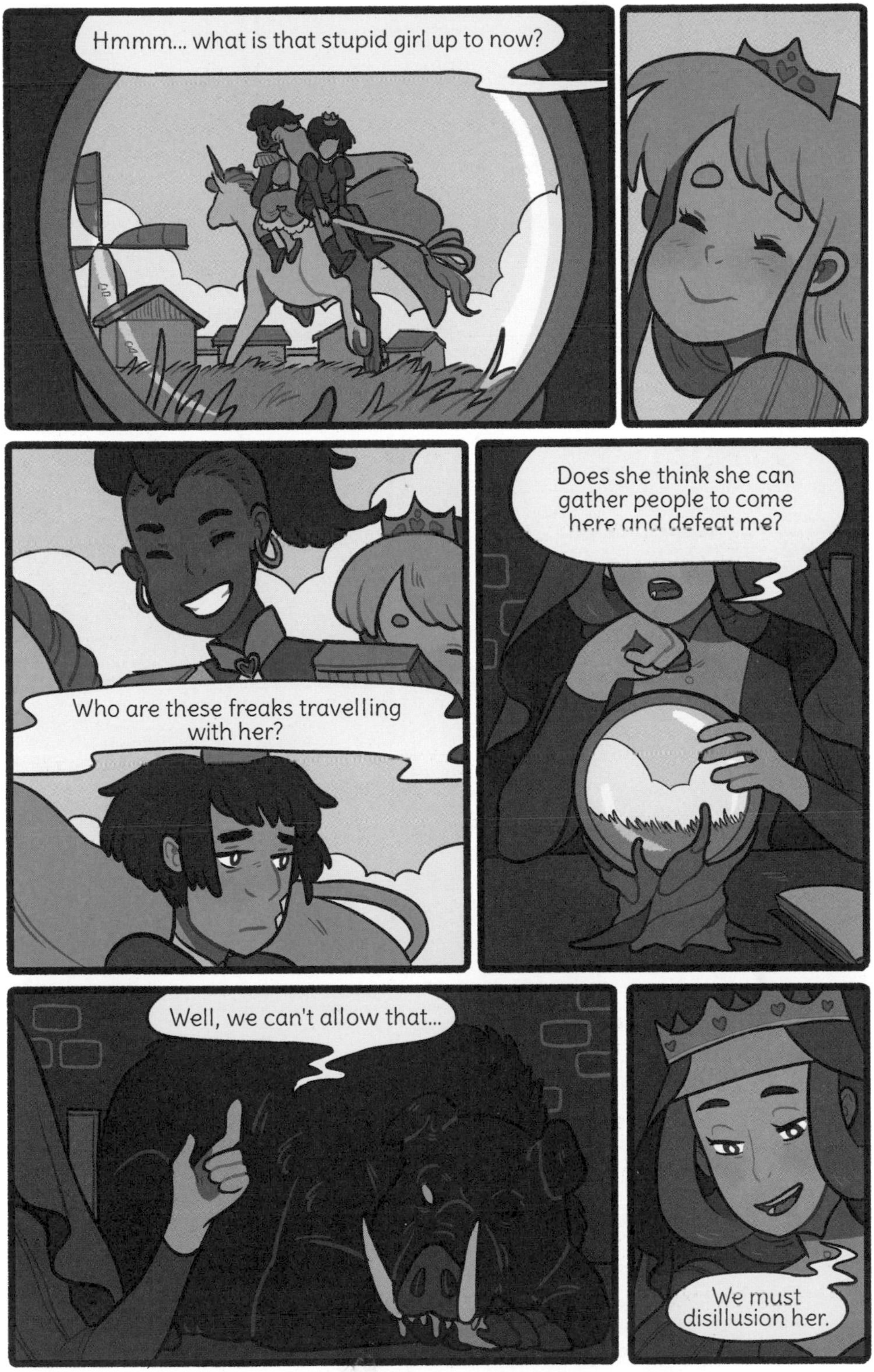
Hmmm... what is that stupid girl up to now?
Who are these freaks travelling with her?
Does she think she can gather people to come here and defeat me?
Well, we can't allow that...
We must disillusion her.

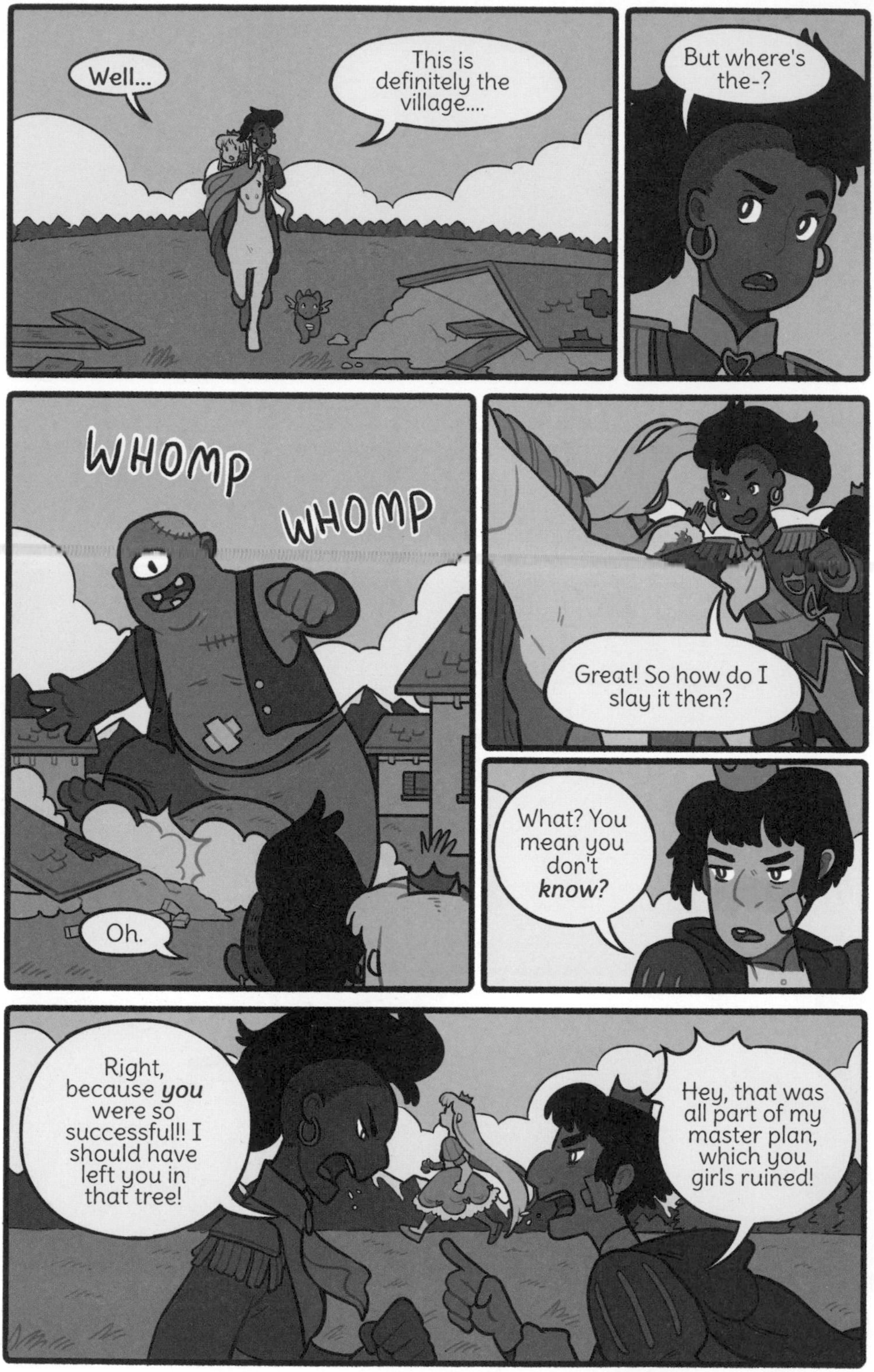
Well...
This is definitely the village....
But where's the-?
WHOMP
WHOMP
Oh.
Great! So how do I slay it then?
What? You mean you don't *know?*
Right, because *you* were so successful!! I should have left you in that tree!
Hey, that was all part of my master plan, which you girls ruined!

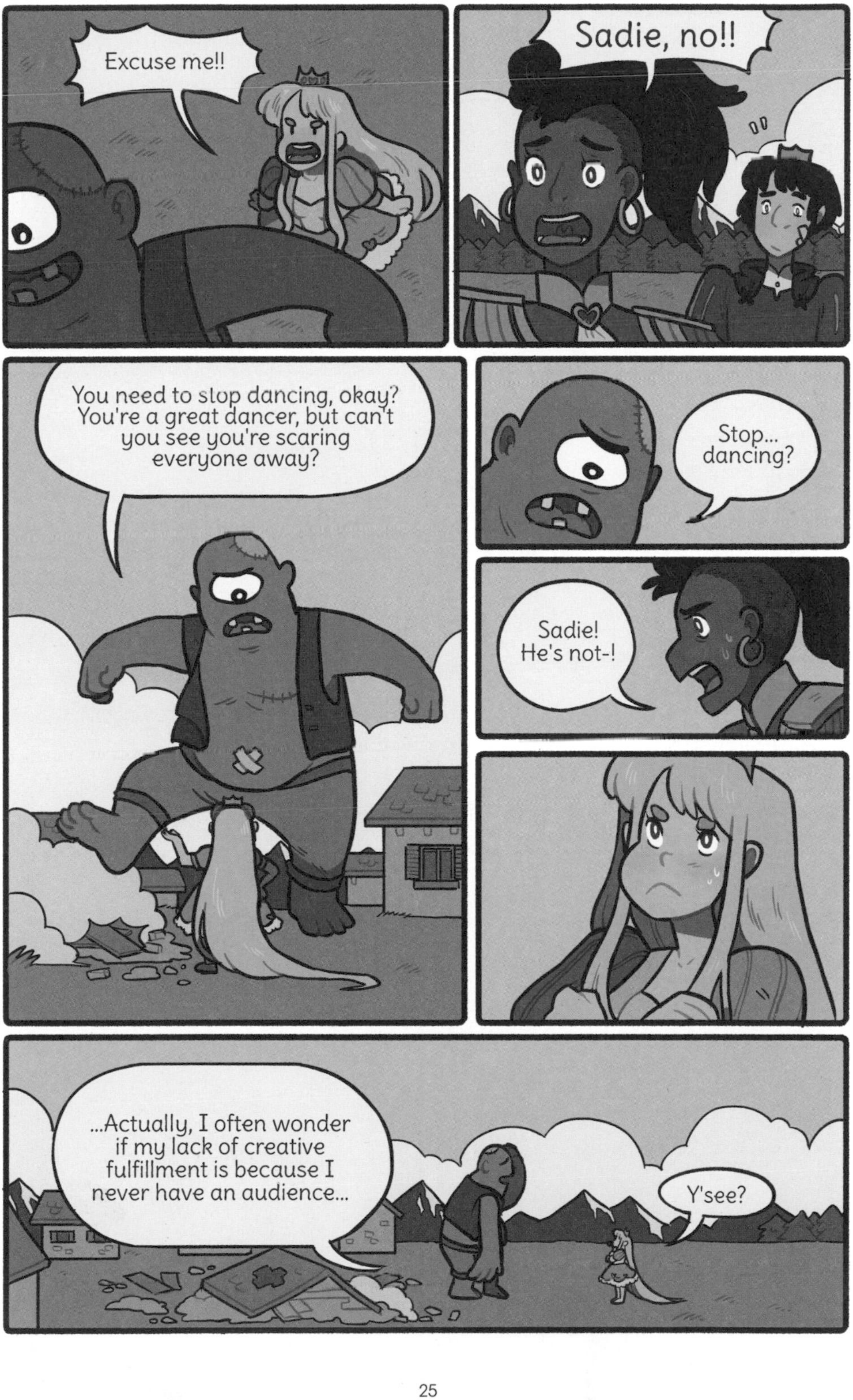
Excuse me!!
Sadie, no!!
You need to stop dancing, okay? You're a great dancer, but can't you see you're scaring everyone away?
Stop... dancing?
Sadie! He's not-!
...Actually, I often wonder if my lack of creative fulfillment is because I never have an audience...
Y'see?

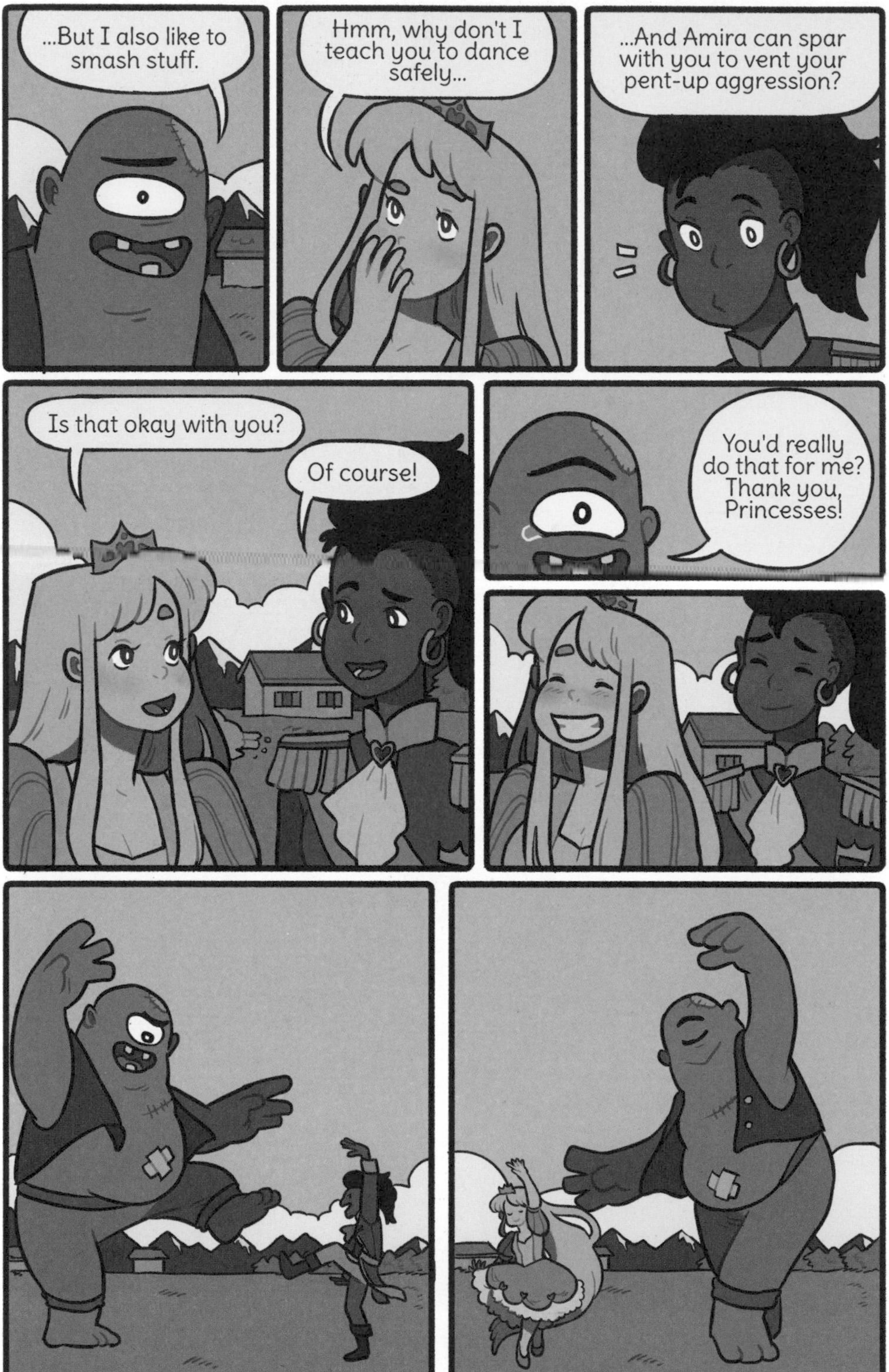
...But I also like to smash stuff.
Hmm, why don't I teach you to dance safely...
...And Amira can spar with you to vent your pent-up aggression?
Is that okay with you?
Of course!
You'd really do that for me? Thank you, Princesses!

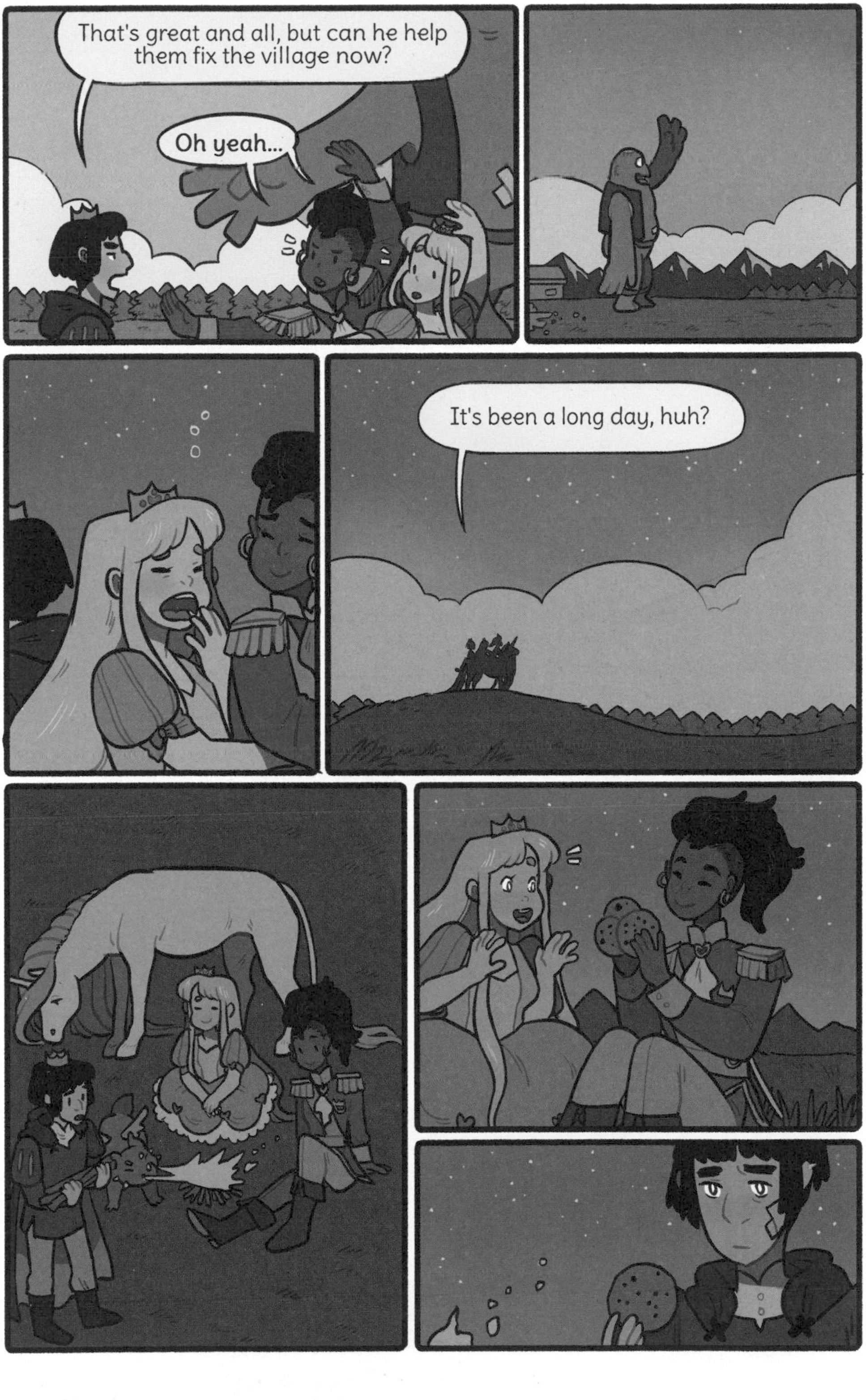
That's great and all, but can he help them fix the village now?
Oh yeah...
It's been a long day, huh?

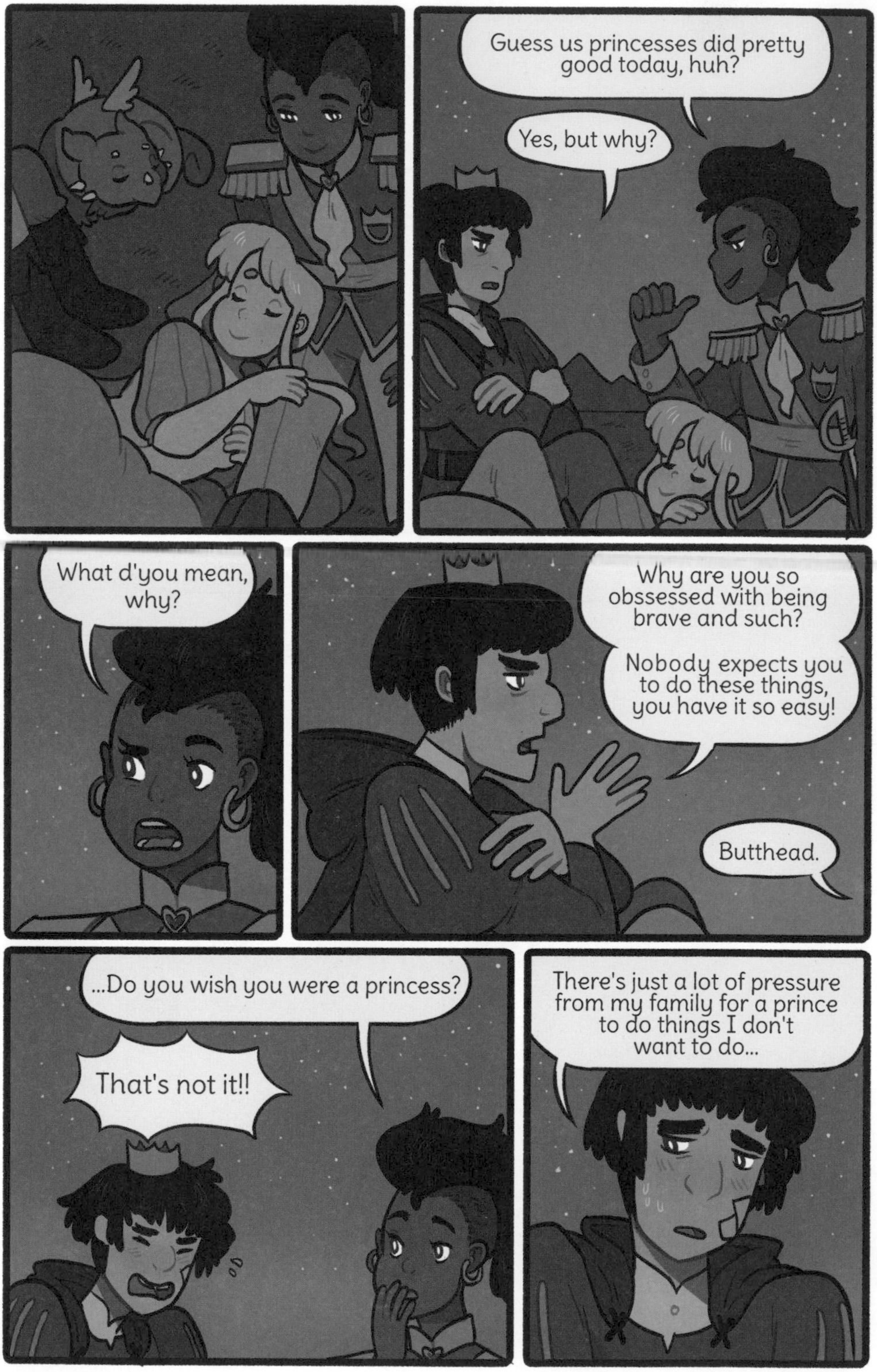
Guess us princesses did pretty good today, huh?
Yes, but why?
What d'you mean, why?
Why are you so obssessed with being brave and such?
Nobody expects you to do these things, you have it so easy!
Butthead.
...Do you wish you were a princess?
That's not it!!
There's just a lot of pressure from my family for a prince to do things I don't want to do...

Like what?

...Like slaying ogres.

Ah. Haha!

Well, I understand parental expectations are hard to deal with...

...But that's no reason to take it out on us.

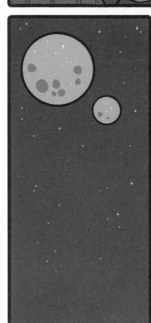

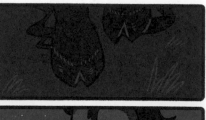

You deserve a cookie too, Celeste.

You again!

I won't let you hurt Sadie!!

HEY!!

Let go of me!!

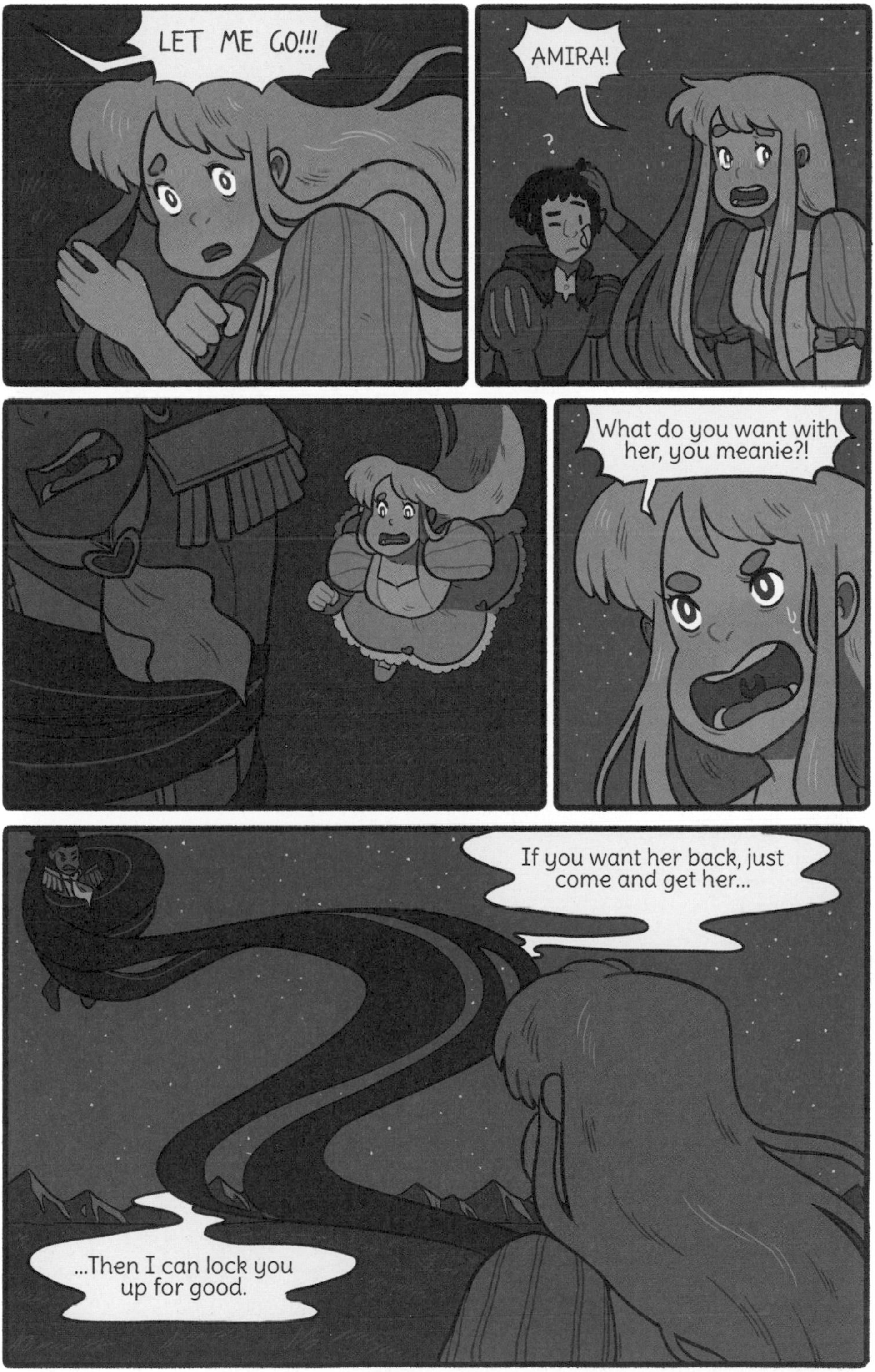

LET ME GO!!!
AMIRA!
?
What do you want with her, you meanie?!
If you want her back, just come and get her...
...Then I can lock you up for good.

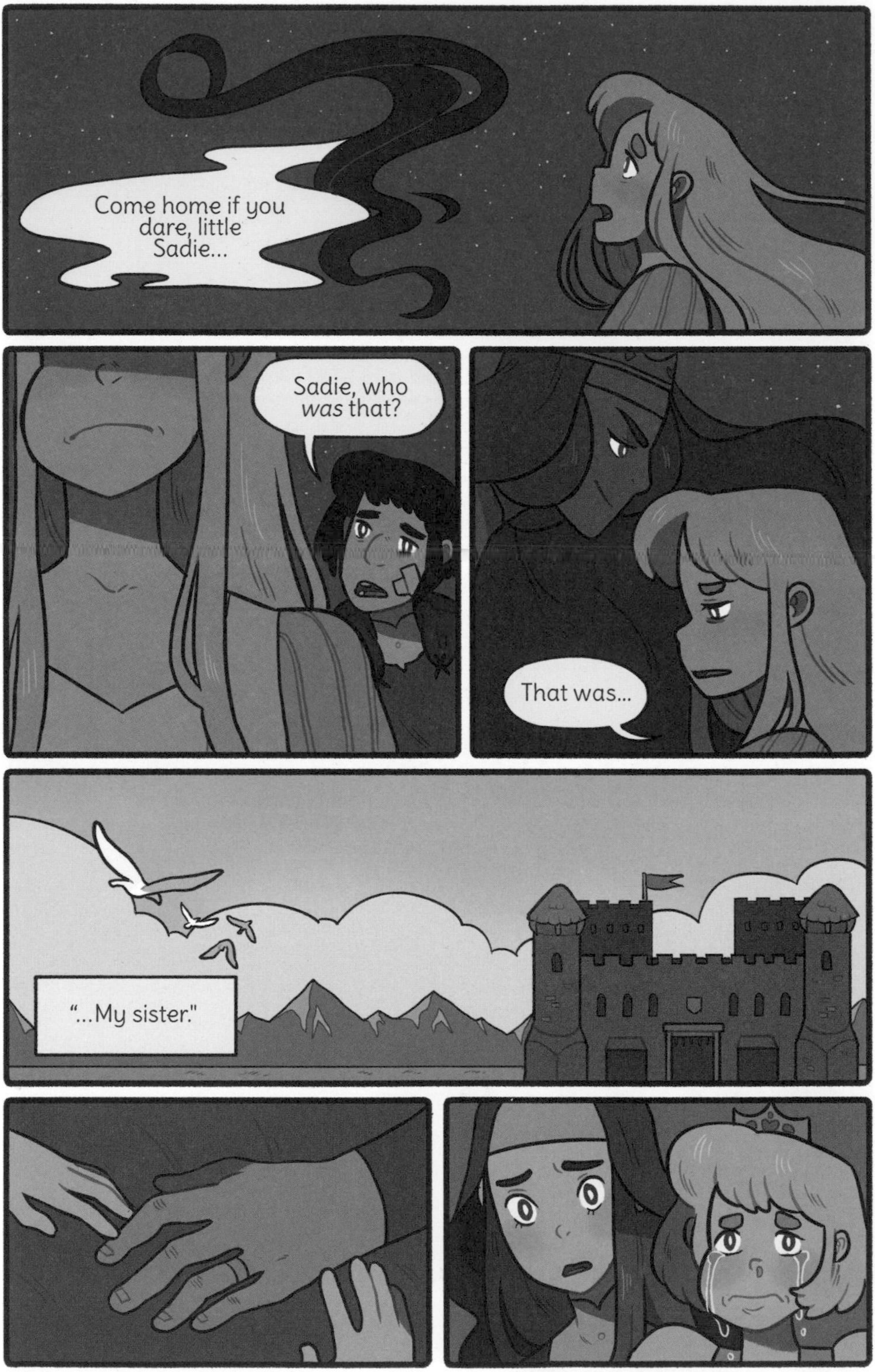

Come home if you dare, little Sadie...
Sadie, who *was* that?
That was...
"...My sister."

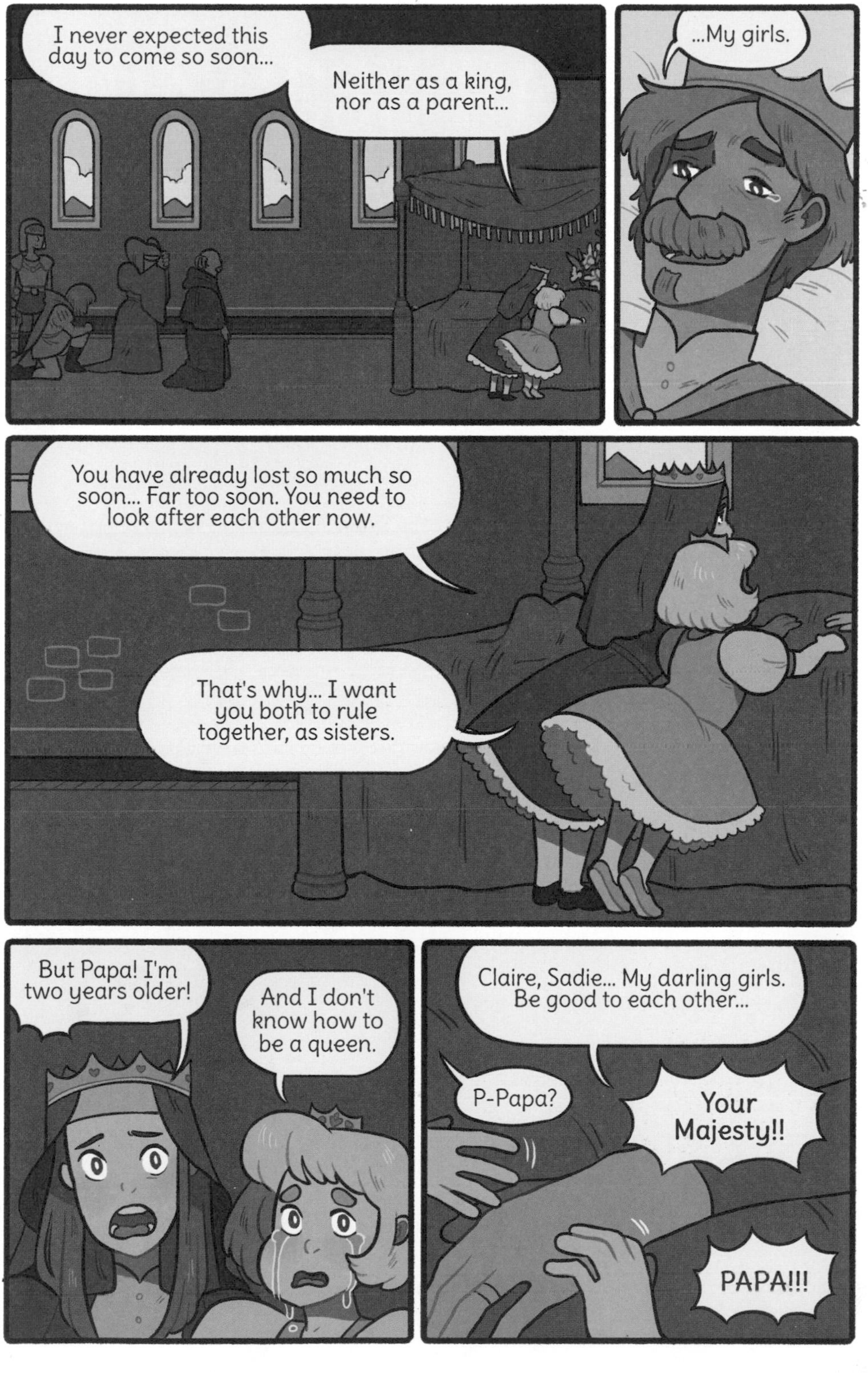
I never expected this day to come so soon...
Neither as a king, nor as a parent...
...My girls.
You have already lost so much so soon... Far too soon. You need to look after each other now.
That's why... I want you both to rule together, as sisters.
But Papa! I'm two years older!
And I don't know how to be a queen.
Claire, Sadie... My darling girls. Be good to each other...
P-Papa?
Your Majesty!!
PAPA!!!

...Papa was wrong, Sadie.

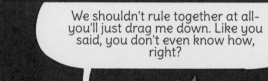
We shouldn't rule together at all— you'll just drag me down. Like you said, you don't even know how, right?

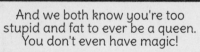

...

And we both know you're too stupid and fat to ever be a queen. You don't even have magic!

Wouldn't it be better for the kingdom if you just... disappeared?

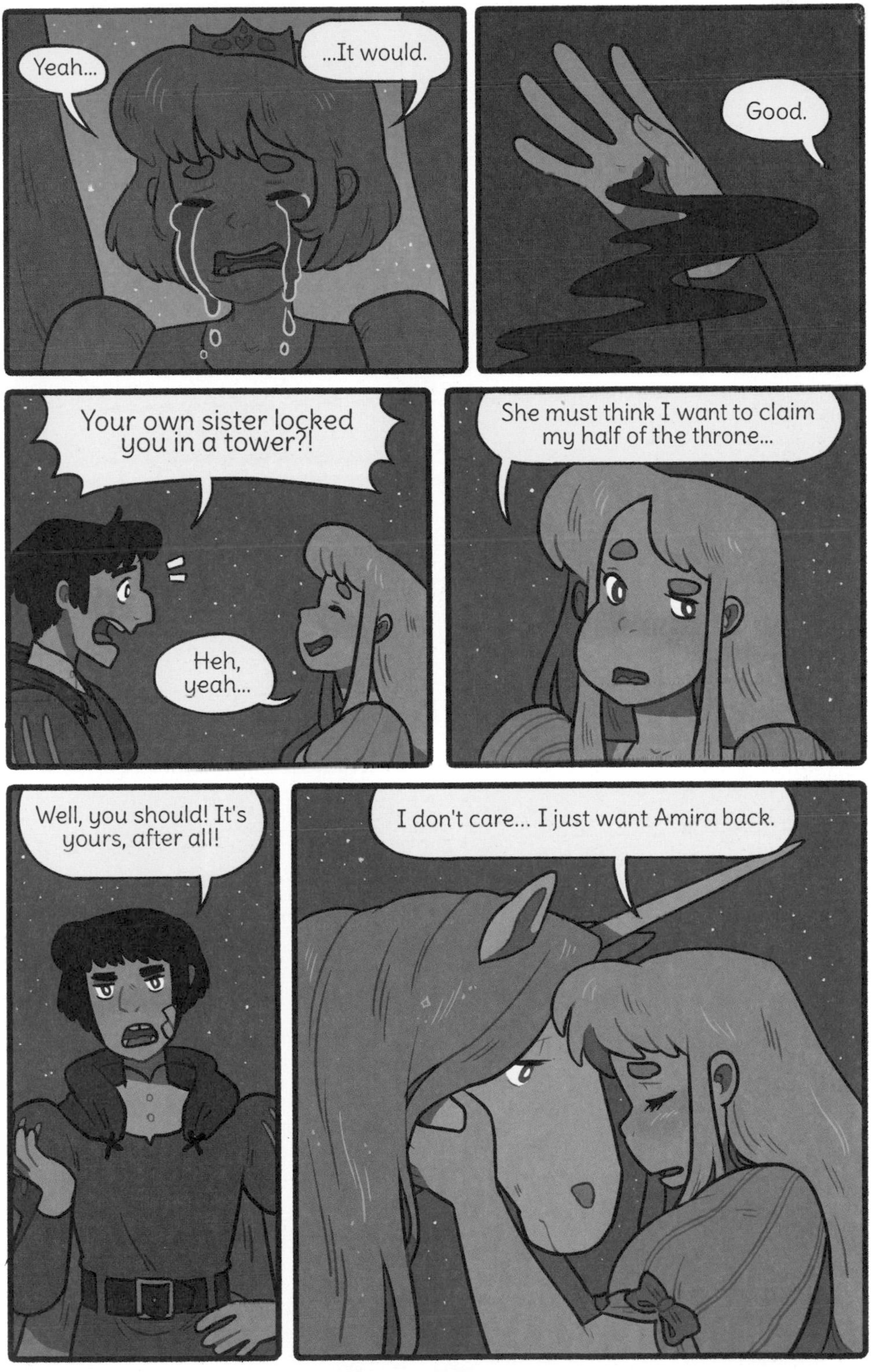
Yeah...
...It would.
Good.
Your own sister locked you in a tower?!
Heh, yeah...
She must think I want to claim my half of the throne...
Well, you should! It's yours, after all!
I don't care... I just want Amira back.

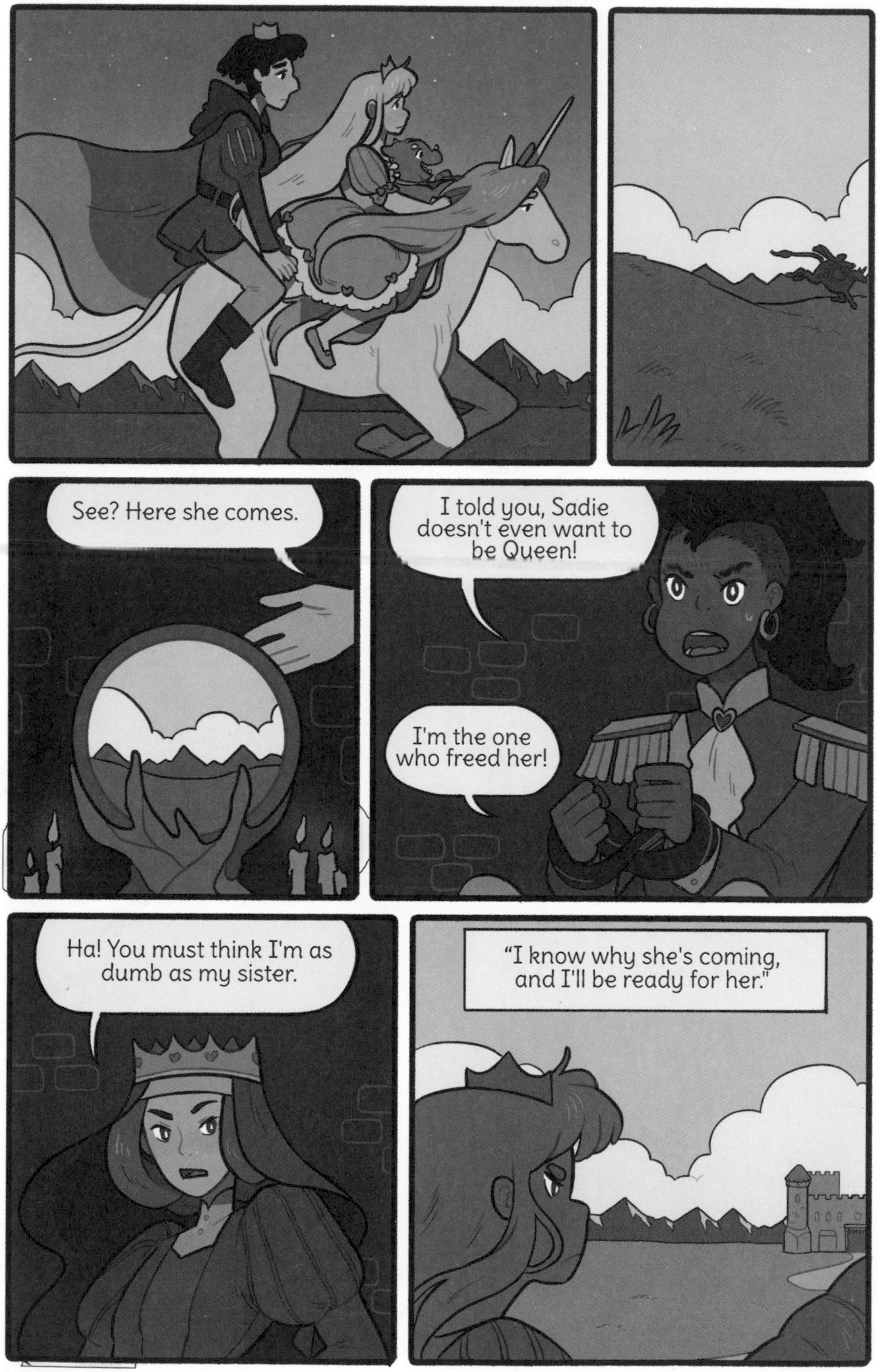
See? Here she comes.
I told you, Sadie doesn't even want to be Queen!
I'm the one who freed her!
Ha! You must think I'm as dumb as my sister.
"I know why she's coming, and I'll be ready for her."

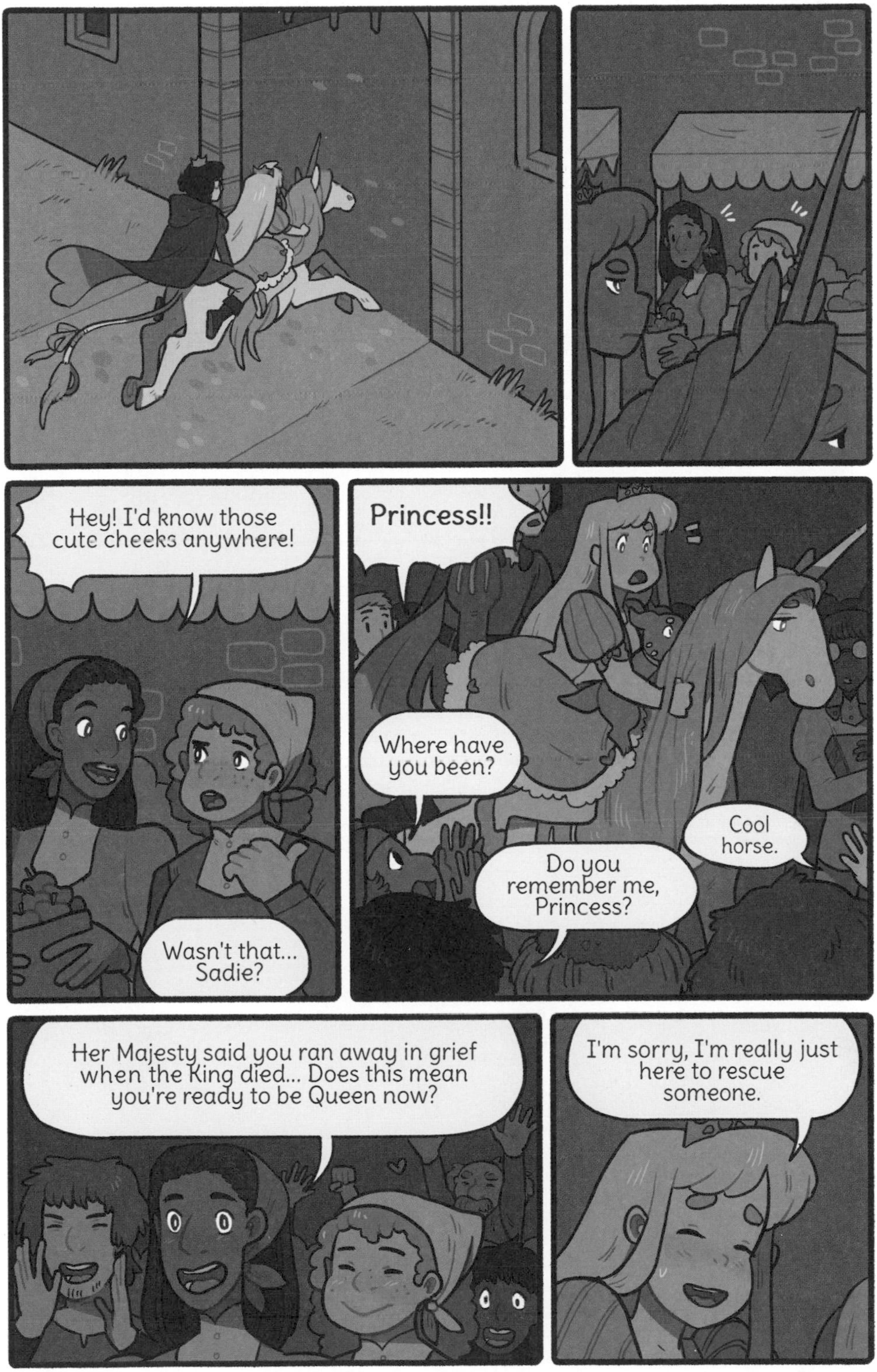
Hey! I'd know those cute cheeks anywhere!
Wasn't that... Sadie?
Princess!!
Where have you been?
Do you remember me, Princess?
Cool horse.
Her Majesty said you ran away in grief when the King died... Does this mean you're ready to be Queen now?
I'm sorry, I'm really just here to rescue someone.

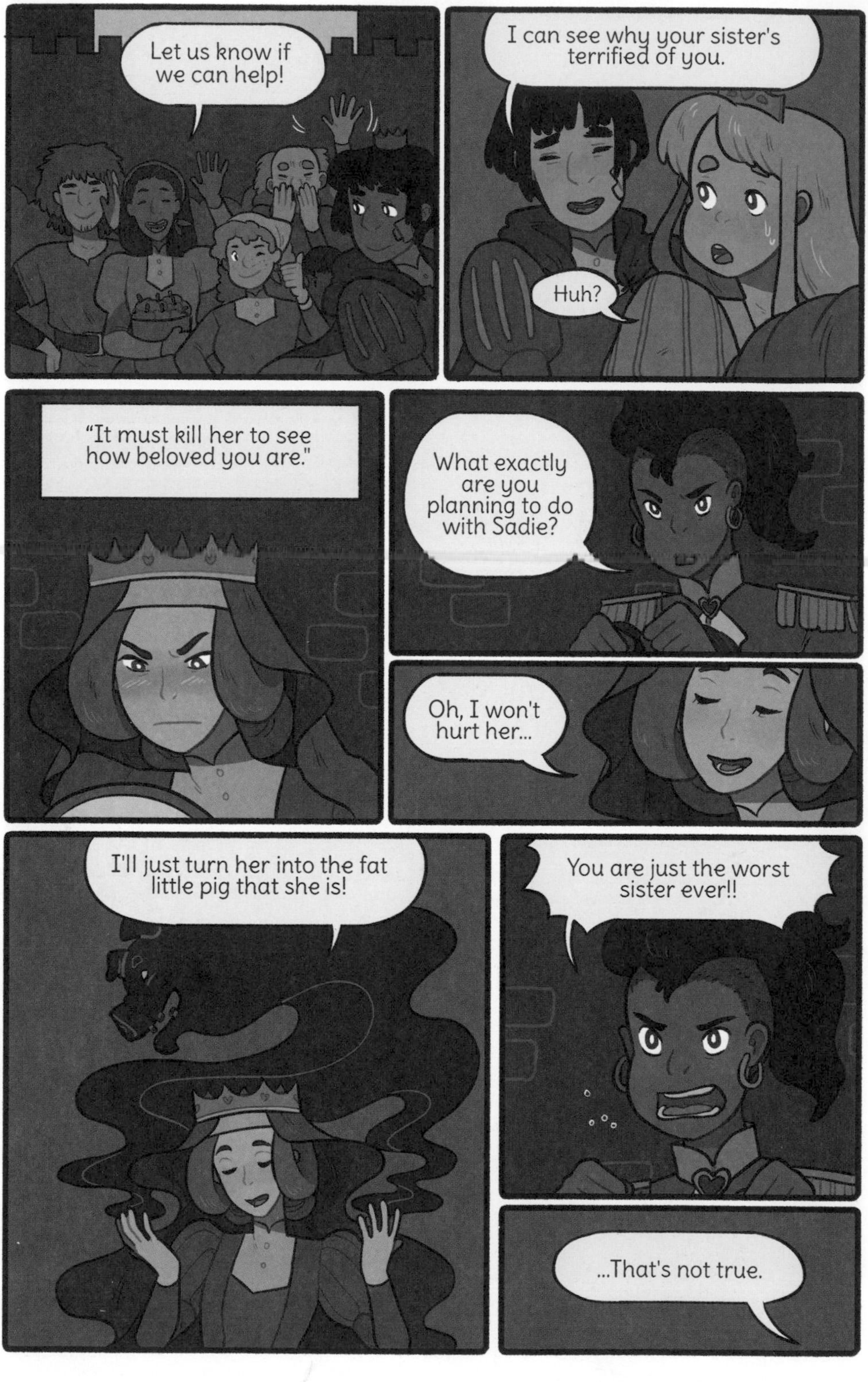
Let us know if we can help!
I can see why your sister's terrified of you.
Huh?
"It must kill her to see how beloved you are."
What exactly are you planning to do with Sadie?
Oh, I won't hurt her...
I'll just turn her into the fat little pig that she is!
You are just the worst sister ever!!
...That's not true.

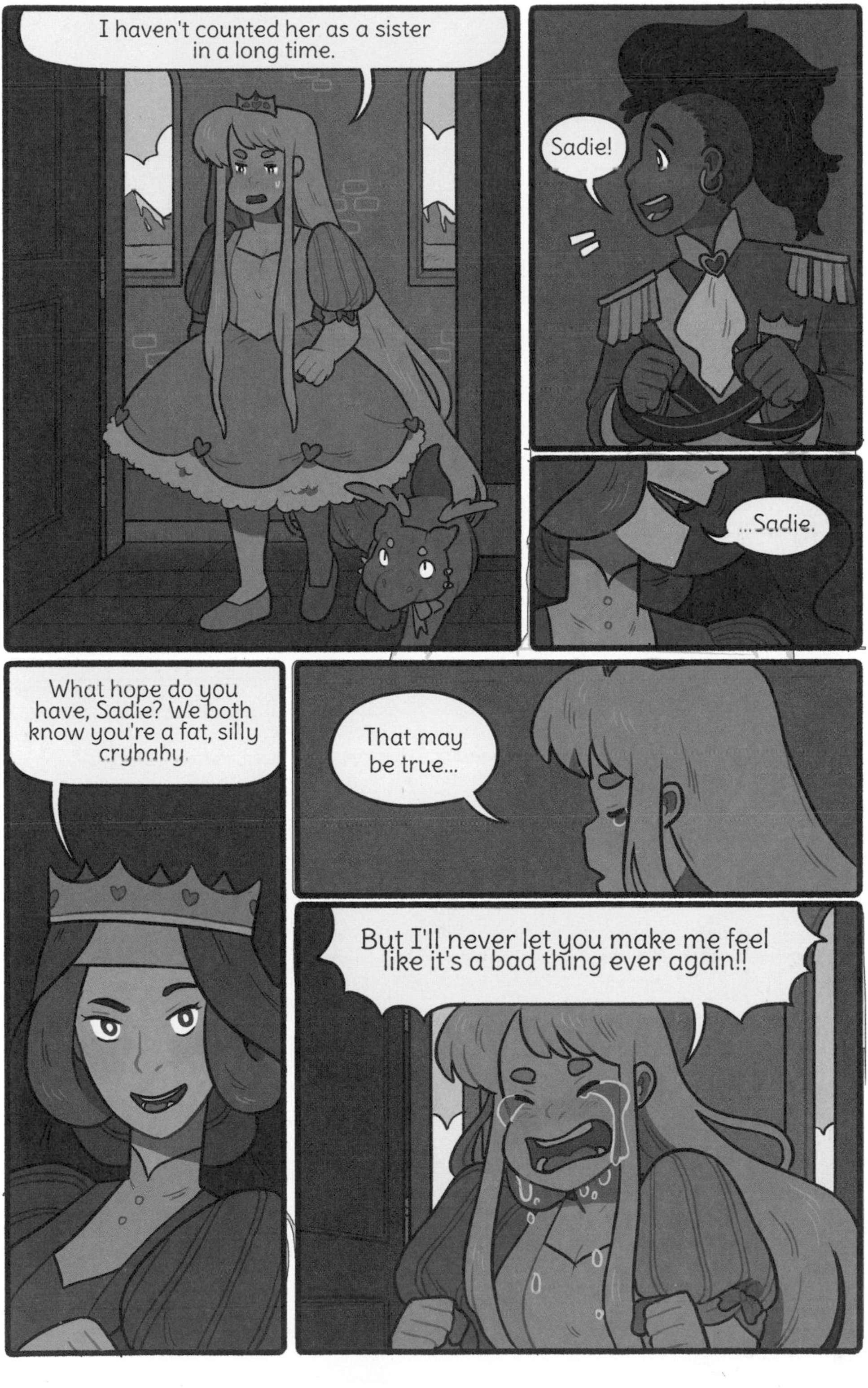

I haven't counted her as a sister in a long time.
Sadie!
...Sadie.
What hope do you have, Sadie? We both know you're a fat, silly crybaby.
That may be true...
But I'll never let you make me feel like it's a bad thing ever again!!

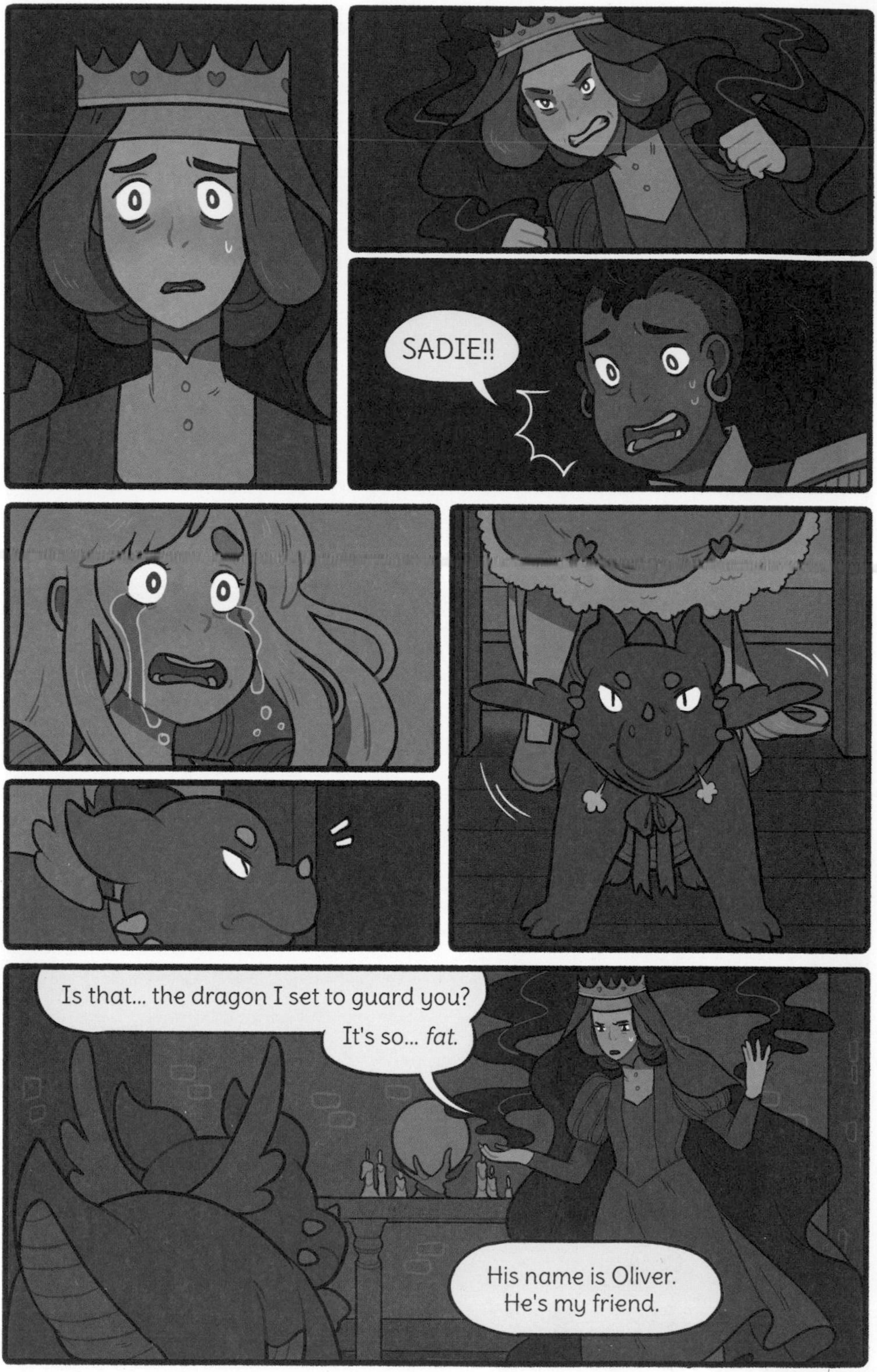
SADIE!!
Is that... the dragon I set to guard you?
It's so... *fat.*
His name is Oliver.
He's my friend.

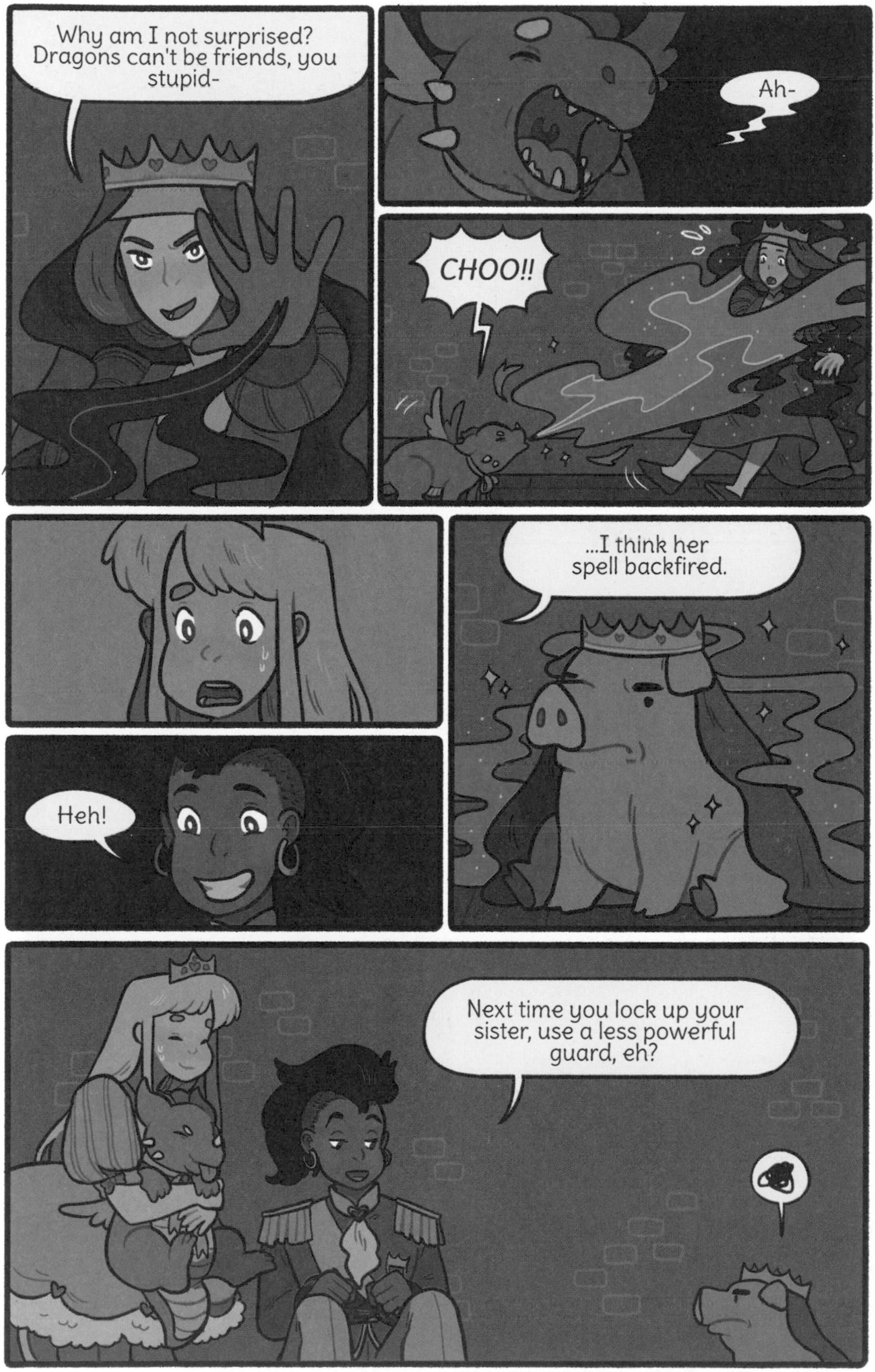
Why am I not surprised? Dragons can't be friends, you stupid-
Ah-
CHOO!!
...I think her spell backfired.
Heh!
Next time you lock up your sister, use a less powerful guard, eh?

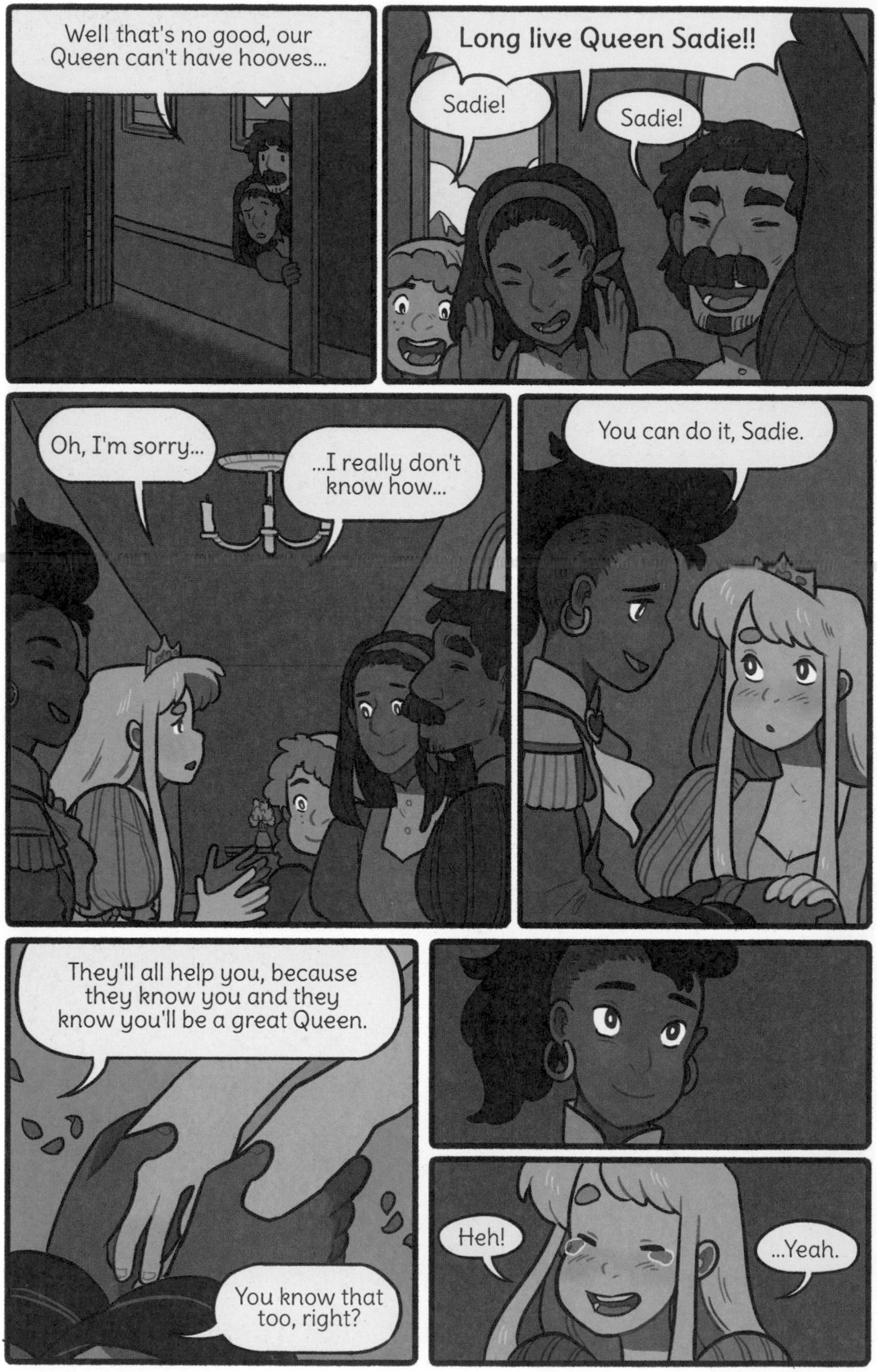
Well that's no good, our Queen can't have hooves...
Long live Queen Sadie!!
Sadie!
Sadie!
Oh, I'm sorry...
...I really don't know how...
You can do it, Sadie.
They'll all help you, because they know you and they know you'll be a great Queen.
You know that too, right?
Heh!
...Yeah.

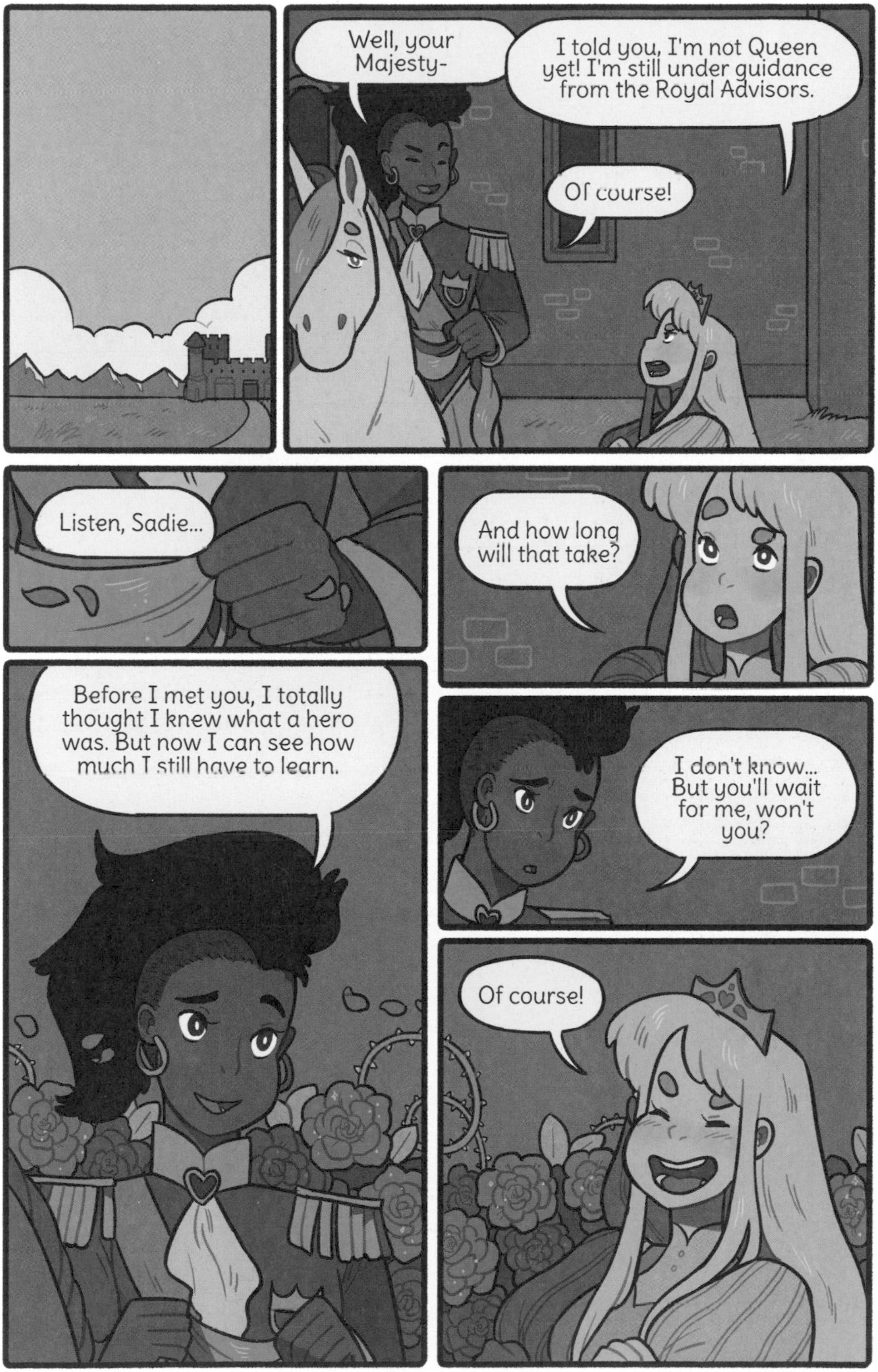

Well, your Majesty-
I told you, I'm not Queen yet! I'm still under guidance from the Royal Advisors.
Of course!
Listen, Sadie...
And how long will that take?
Before I met you, I totally thought I knew what a hero was. But now I can see how much I still have to learn.
I don't know... But you'll wait for me, won't you?
Of course!

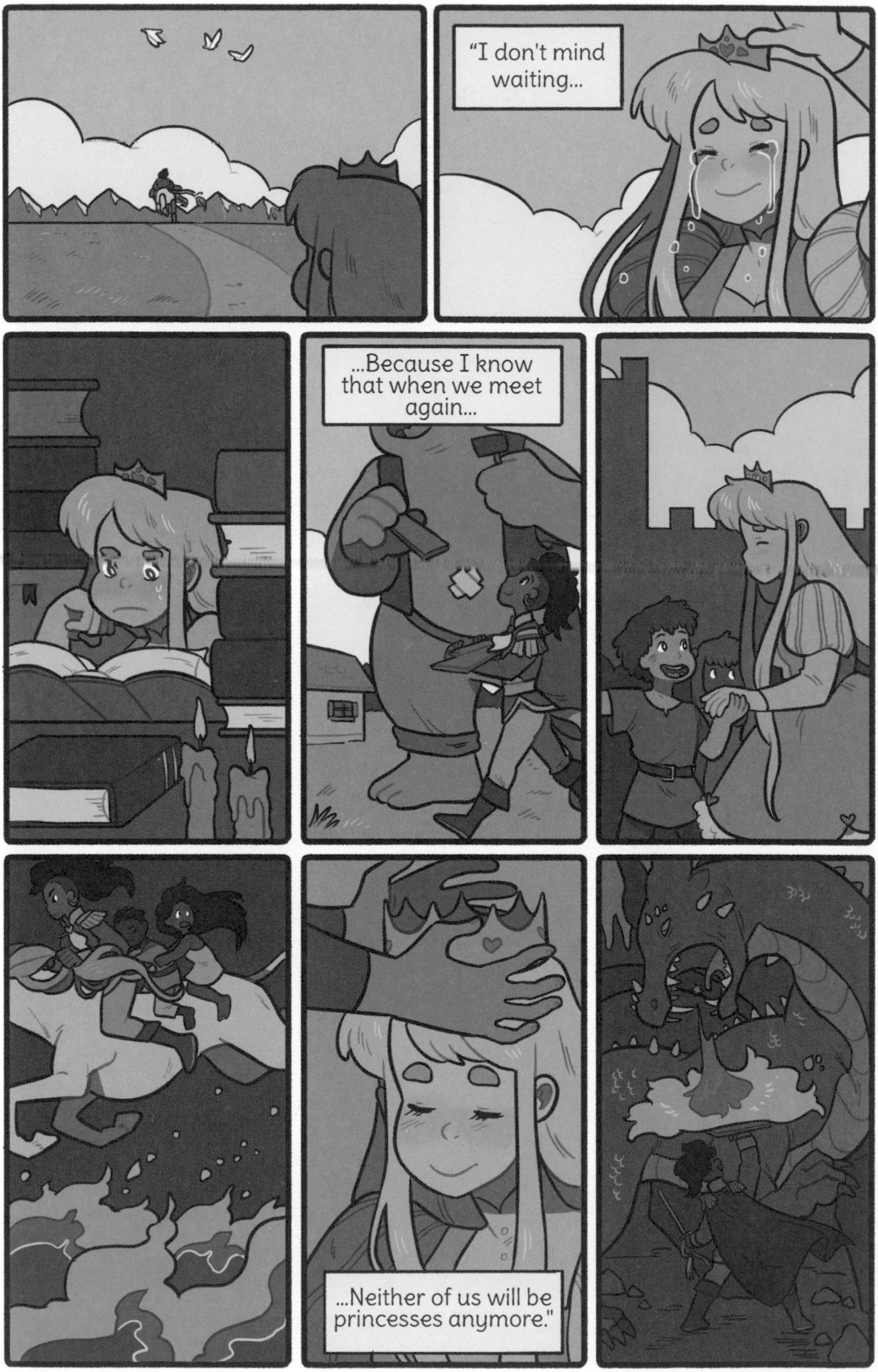
"I don't mind waiting...
...Because I know that when we meet again...
...Neither of us will be princesses anymore."

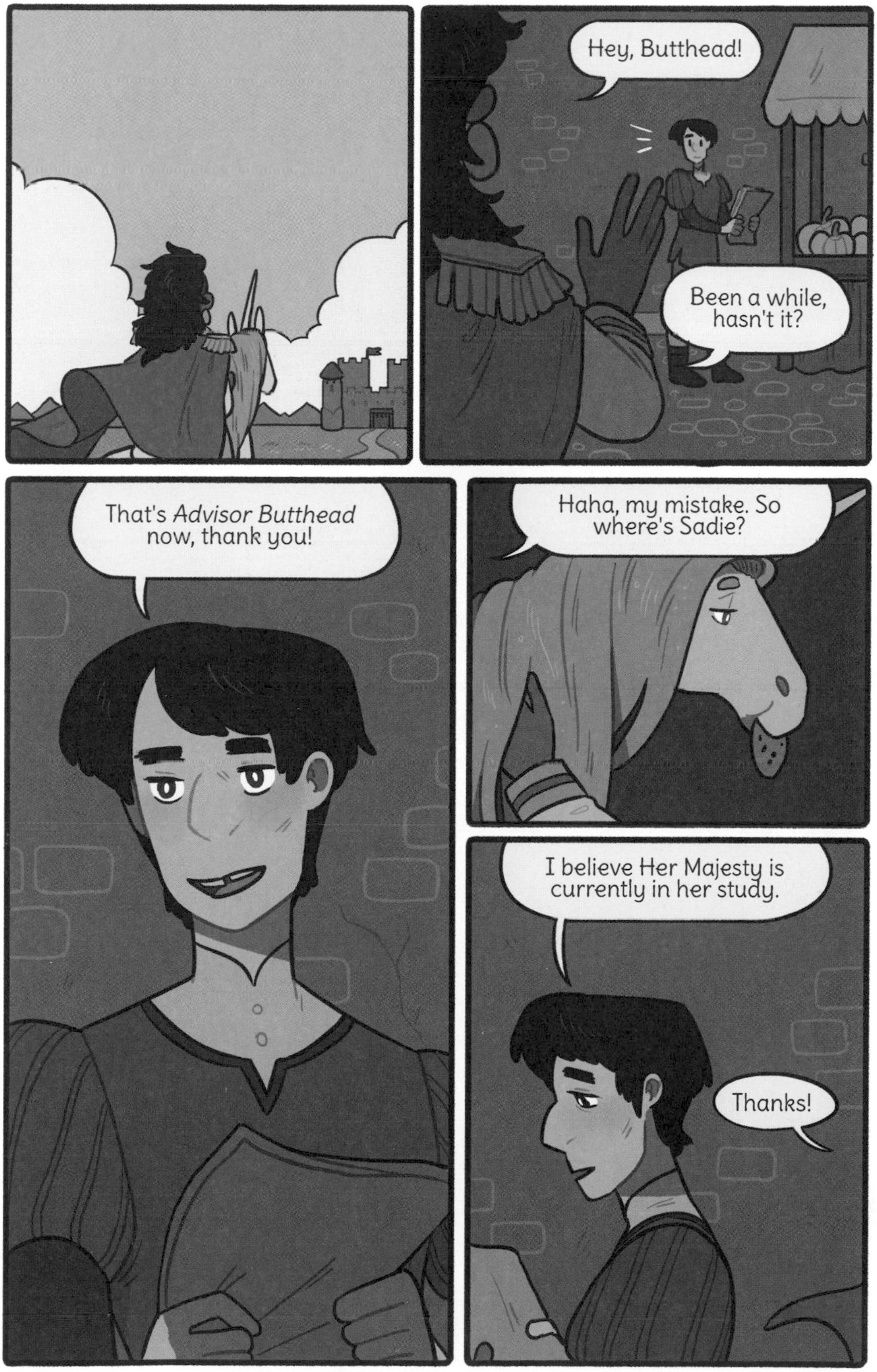
Hey, Butthead!
Been a while, hasn't it?
That's *Advisor Butthead* now, thank you!
Haha, my mistake. So where's Sadie?
I believe Her Majesty is currently in her study.
Thanks!

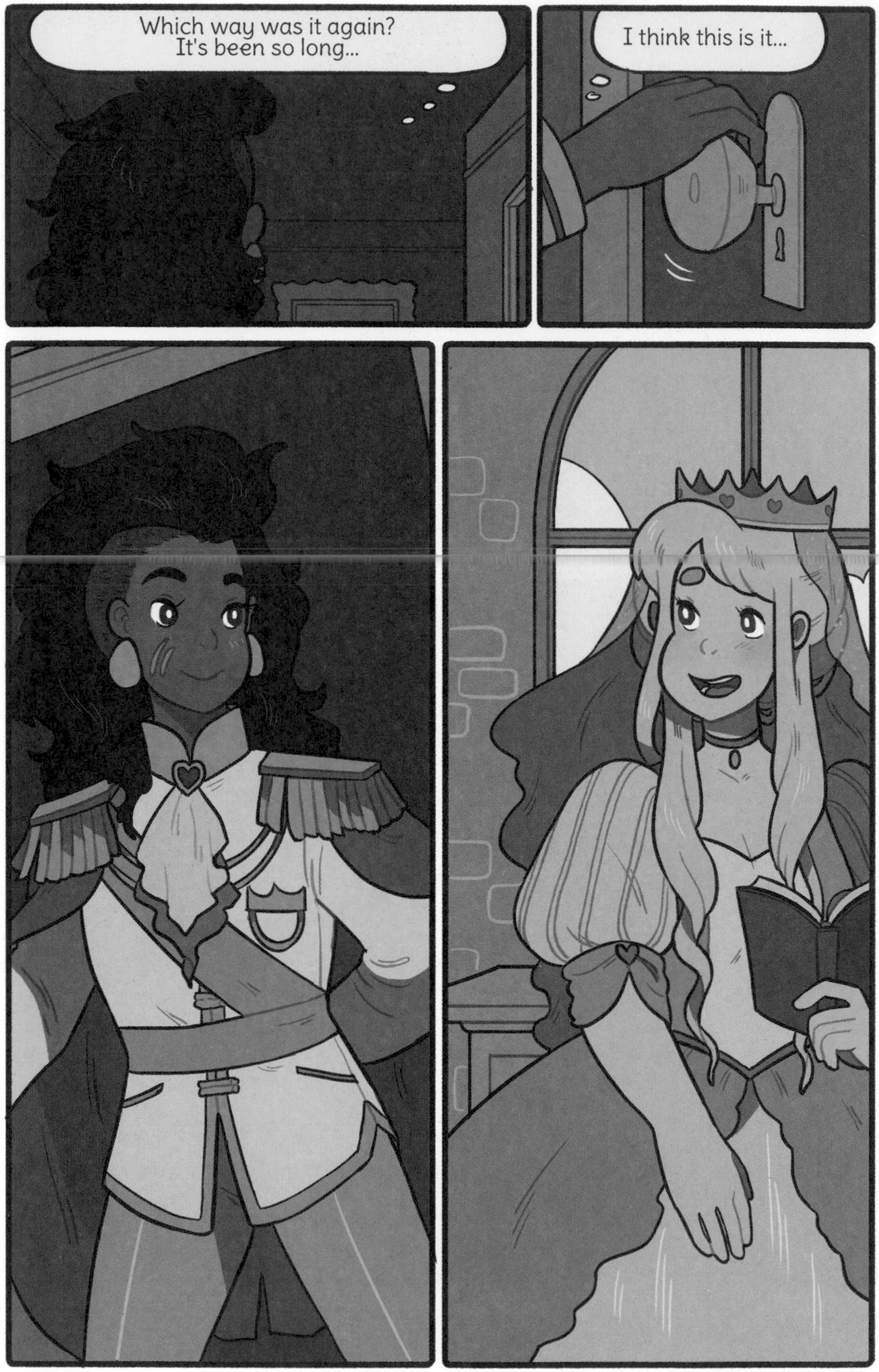
Which way was it again? It's been so long...
I think this is it...

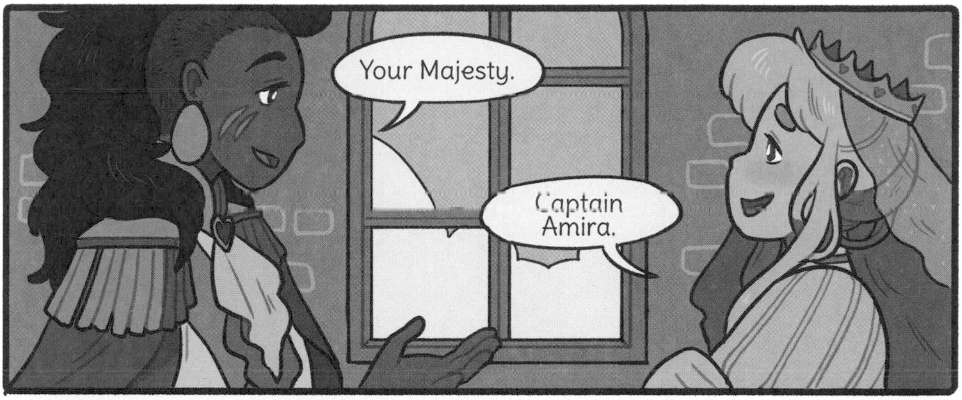
Your Majesty.
Captain Amira.

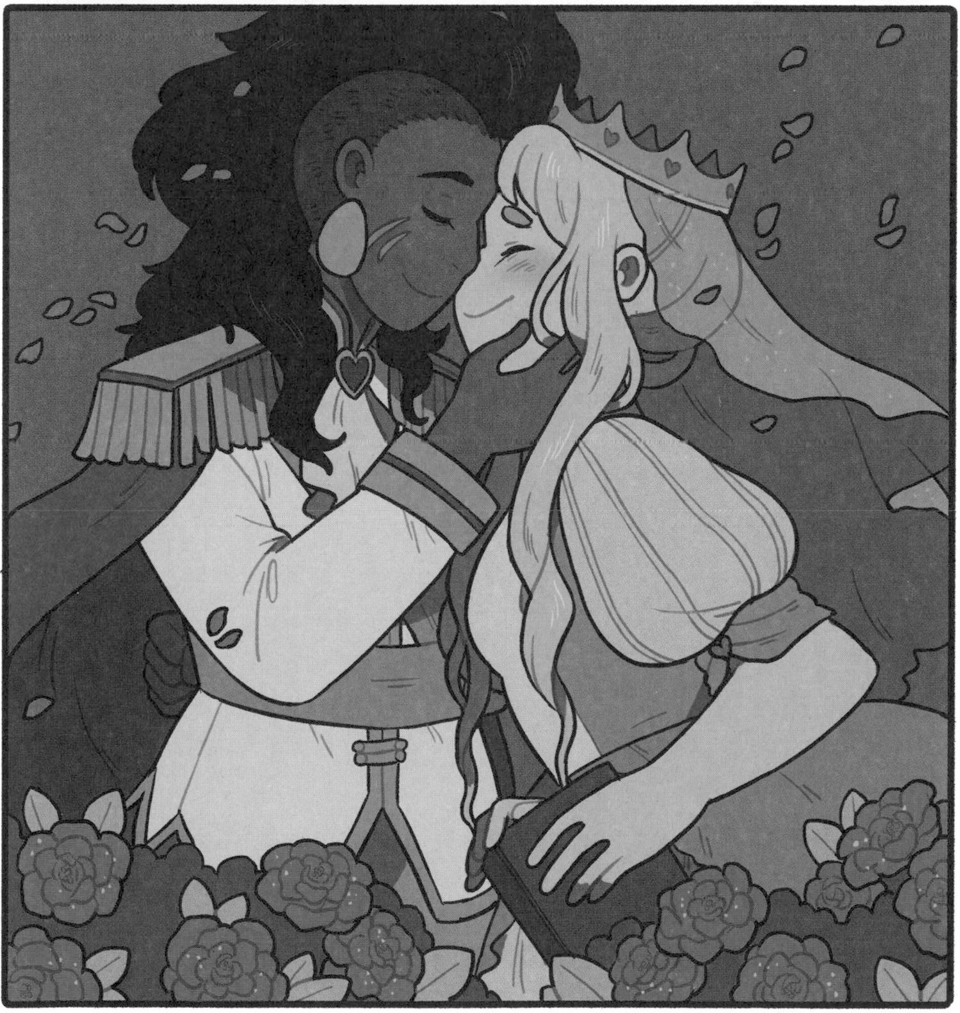

The End

Epilogue

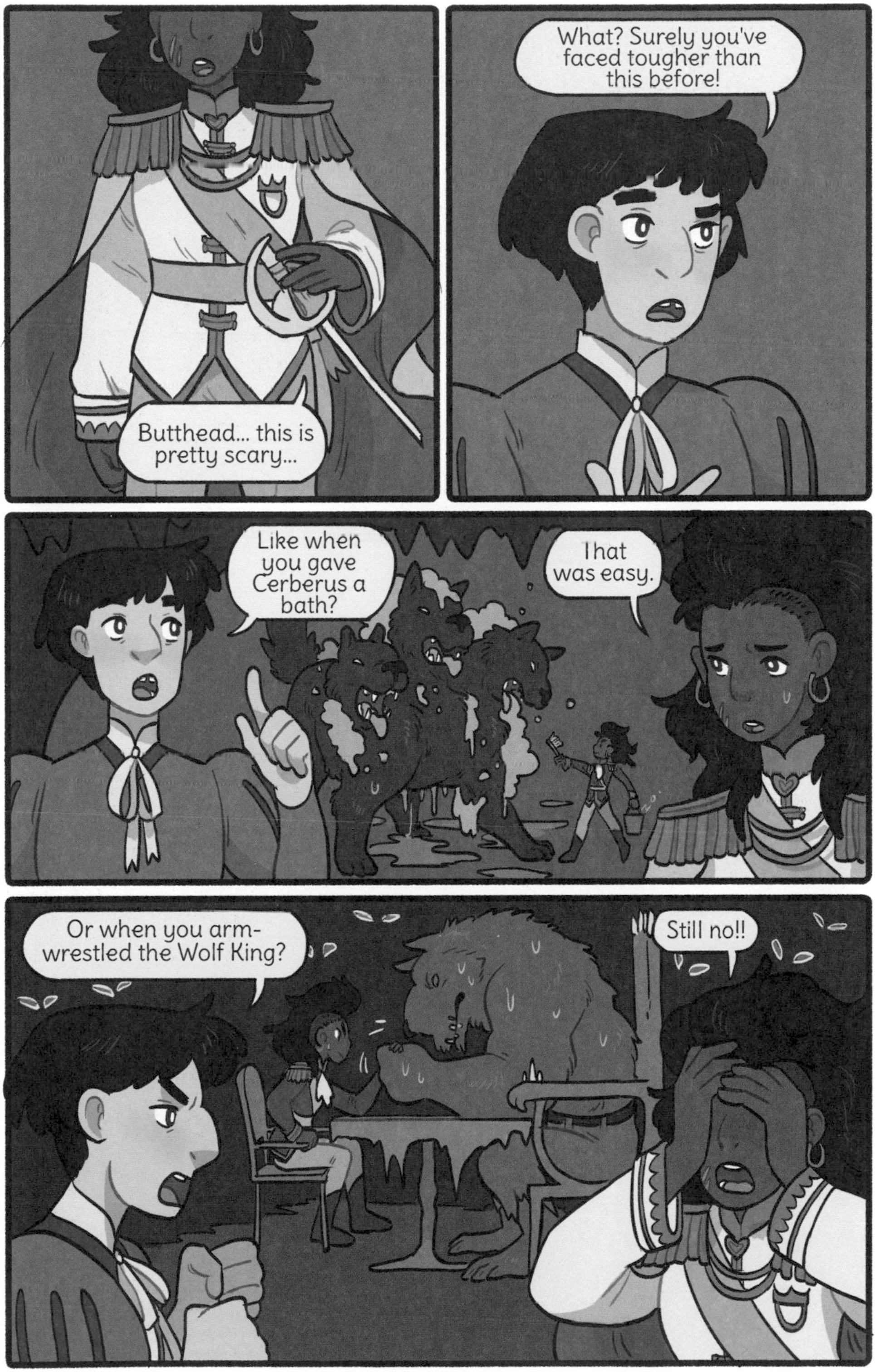
Butthead... this is pretty scary...
What? Surely you've faced tougher than this before!
Like when you gave Cerberus a bath?
That was easy.
Or when you arm-wrestled the Wolf King?
Still no!!

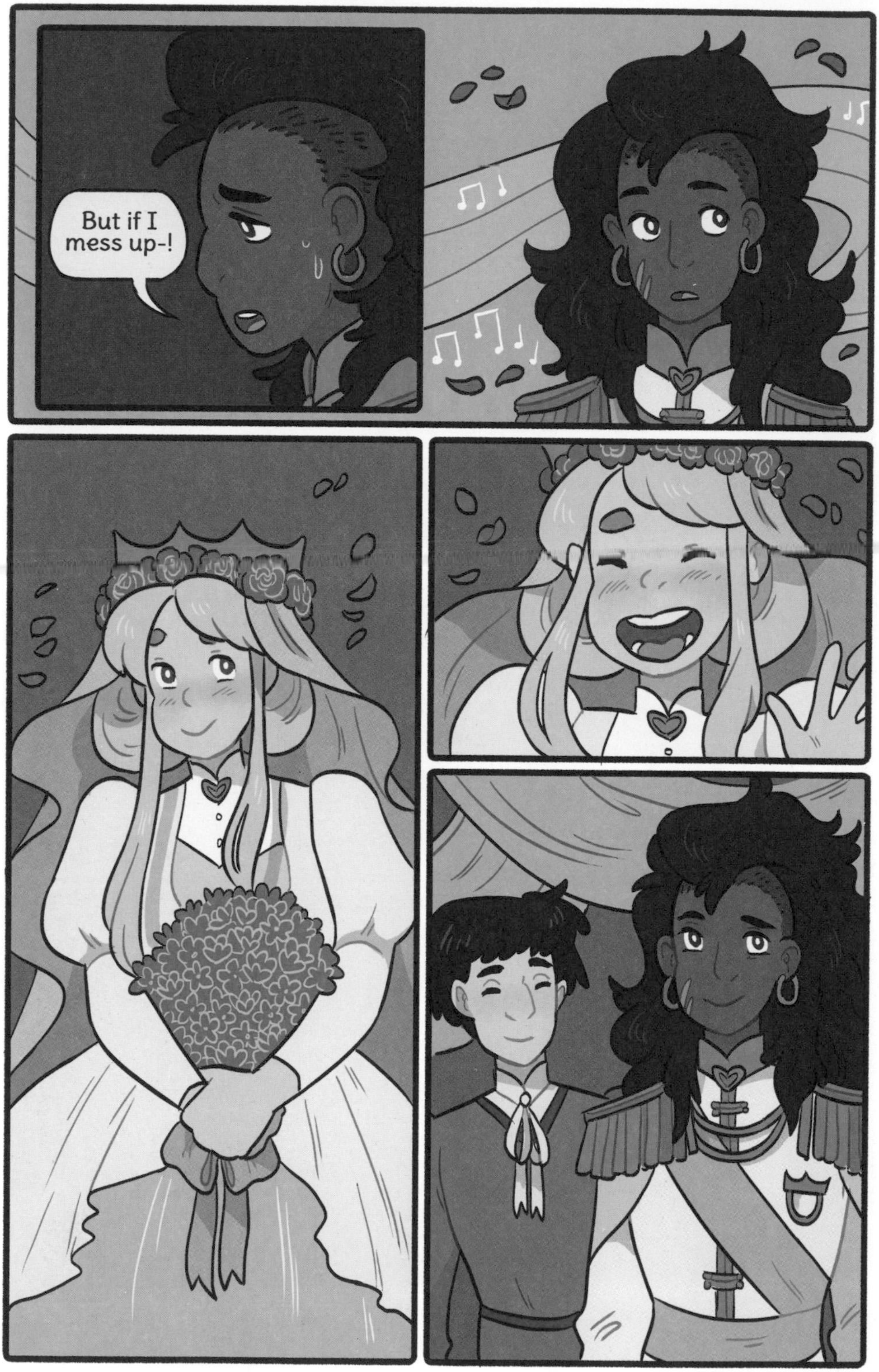
But if I mess up-!

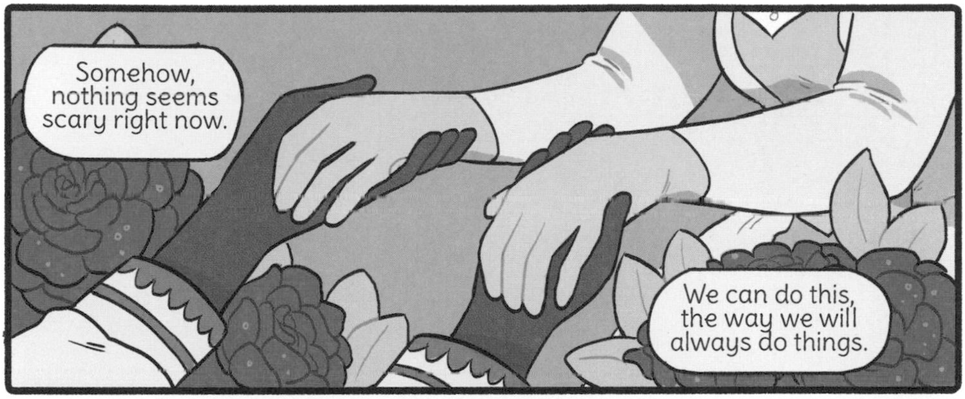
Somehow, nothing seems scary right now.
We can do this, the way we will always do things.

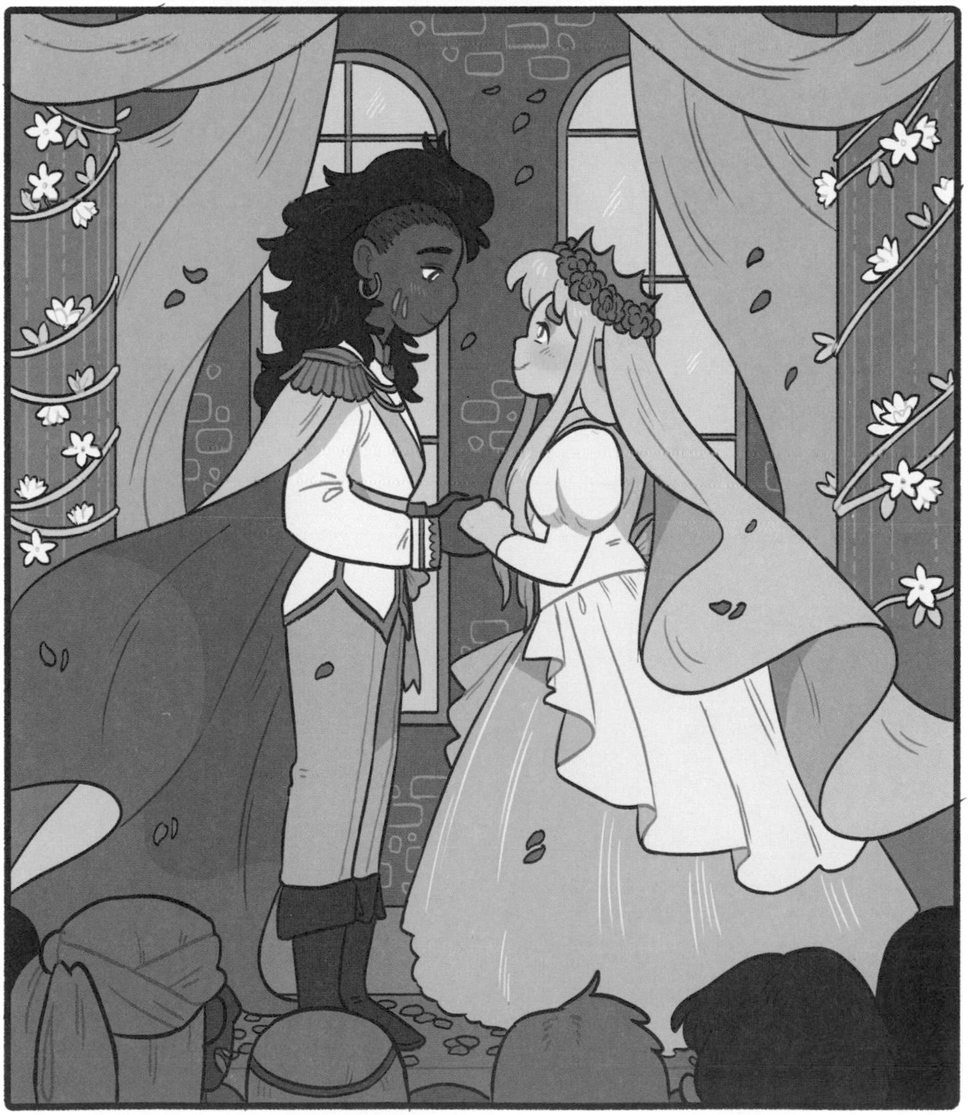

Katie is a writer and illustrator from New Zealand. Currently she lives with her cat, Arthur, who is an awful lot like Oliver. You can find more of her work at strangelykatie.com.

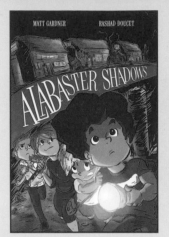

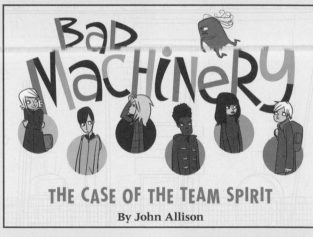